IRINA

June gave a sharp cry and started to swing her legs over the low fire escape, staring down blindly at the concrete seven floors below. Irina felt her heartbeat quicken. Her senses dizzied.

"Don't try to stop me," June shrilled. "You've stolen Phil from me and I don't want to live."

Irina stood locked, motionless, thinking, *What a kick! What a bang! What a sweet, unique, ice-cold thrill, watching somebody's last few seconds of life, seeing it and feeling close up.* Her head ached. There's never been anything like this. *Does June have the guts to go through with it? Do I, Irina, have the guts to* let *her do it . . . ?*

AUTHOR'S PROFILE

Recognized as one of America's outstanding contemporary novelists, Stuart Friedman began his writing career in 1938 after first trying his luck in the advertising field, working as a real estate agent and heading up the operation of a labor-industry counseling service.

Born in the mid-West, Mr. Friedman devoted his first writing efforts to the publication of a comprehensive history of the State of Indiana. Since that first venture, he has written more than a dozen novels and hundreds of stories and articles for leading national magazines.

One of Monarch Books' top selling authors with sales of more than 2 million copies overall, he is, perhaps, best known for his current favorites RASPUTIN: THE MAD MONK, RAVAGED and THE FLY GIRLS.

A Contemporary Novel

IRINA

Stuart Friedman

Author of RAVAGED and
THE FLY GIRLS

WILDSIDE PRESS

For
Jeanette

Cover Painting by Tom Miller

chapter one

Irina's senses were nakedly alive as she raced down the dangerous mountain highway in her low-slung, open Jaguar. An intense young beauty flamboyantly costumed in goggles, blue-green-white knit mask, glossy yellow hooded parka and bright red stretch pants, she loved the feel of speed and power. She drove like a night huntress, spearing slower cars with the black Jag's long white-blazing headlights, then dropping them behind her like small game.

Ten minutes after take-off from Sky Hi Ski Lodge she sped out of a turn into a straight, shallow downgrade, caught sight of the big game and grinned. Jamming the accelerator to the floor, she swung across the center line and disposed of the final car separating her from the stubby little white Porsche. Its top was cozily closed.

"The lovers!" Irina thought sardonically, watching the Porsche scoot out of sight around the next turn. "How sweet!"

She laughed and hit the turn to the right in a tire-shrieking skid that carried the heavy, overpowered machine to the left shoulder of the road. Powering out of the skid she slashed back across into her own lane an instant before an approaching car climbed into view.

The road looped in a descending left turn around a towering outthrust of the mountain. Beyond the right shoulder was emptiness, a drop of hundreds of feet. The downgrade increased the Jag's speeding momentum and her gloved hands clutched the wheel, fighting the strong pull to the right. But the ball and toes of one shoeless foot remained delicately posed on the accelerator a fraction of a second too long. When she lifted her foot the car didn't slow.

Tensing, Irina resisted the deadly temptation to brake suddenly. Distantly she was aware of endless ghostly miles of high Sierra like some harshly beautiful moonscape of stone and snow and forest and awesome black gorges. Immediately ahead, rushing at her, she saw little posts and cables at the edge of the chasm like toothpicks and string against the Jag's mass.

Her right wheels went off the pavement, then her left. The car hurtling sidewards out of control, swiftly consuming the few yards of rough ground between the road and the little fence. Irina was abruptly certain she was going to crash through and pitch down helplessly through space.

Sometimes when she flew, wingless, off the lip of a ski jump the chill-and-fever mixture of fear and sexual sensation made her expell her breath explosively in a piercing laugh-scream. Now, her breath stopped. Behind mask and goggles was a paralyzed smile and a stark glaze over her vivid eyes. She saw herself defenseless and lovely in a satin-lined casket while her stepfather gazed down at her.

She felt the tail of the Jag whipping toward the fence. For just a moment the nose was aimed at the road. She stomped the accelerator down to the floor just before the rear of the car smashed into a post, raising sparks. The tires cut down like grinding wheels, grooving the earth and flinging a shower of stone fragments and sod out into the chasm. But the whole car was moving inexorably backward . . . then the wheels found traction. The Jag seemed almost to leap to the pavement.

Safe again but shaky, she drove moderately. She thought soberly about the lovers in the white Porsche, both students at her college. Phil Harkness, an engineering postgrad, and June Earlson, within months of her B.A. in education, planned to marry and live tidily ever after. Which was their dismal right, she supposed, even if—or maybe *because*—June was a spineless rabbit and Phil a mock-bold paper tiger. Phil, vigorous and physically skillful, looked good within the framework of properly organized games. He was courageous behind a fence of safe rules because it was play and had no consequences that could affect his total life.

Outside sports he never took a stand or ventured an opinion till he was sure which way the wind was blowing. He shunned campus political battles, controversial issues and everything that had the flavor of defiance of authority. Phil kept his instinctively daring spirit imprisoned and resented anyone's trying to free it. He disliked being roused, which was why Irina had fallen out of love with

6

him and broken their engagement. He had the right girl now and she didn't want him back.

Phil and June were headed for the Reno hotel suite that the gang from college had rented for the weekend and they were counting on an hour alone before any of the others came down from the ski lodge. Her plan to bust things up would be a display of power for the sheer hell of it, Irina knew.

It might be too wild and bitchy even for Irina Devereaux; maybe she ought to call off the chase. Besides, it would subject innocents on the highway to serious danger and might cripple or kill somebody. To continue would be indefensible, morally loathsome.

A corner of her mouth indented in a derisive grin. Her psychology professor would be fascinated to know that one minute after she had had the pants scared off her she started thinking like a good girl. Who said morality wasn't the child of fear? Not Irina, she assured herself. She shifted in the bucket seat and set out after "the lovers."

She sighted the Porsche a third of the way down the next long straightaway. Midway, she was within striking distance and she hung there until Phil began to slow for the approaching turn. Then, hoping to startle or, with luck, anger Phil, she unleashed a burst of speed.

She came up on the Porsche's tail with a sudden roar as if she were going to go right through it. She cut sharply into the left lane, came alongside and stayed there. Pacing the white car exactly, she looked across and waved at Phil. He glanced at her briefly, then tried to ignore her.

A big, emptily handsome man in his early twenties wearing dark sweater, open suede jacket and a knitted black wool cap like an inverted crock on his squarish blond head, Phil sat looking snug and smug. Beside him, in a cuddly coat with a fur-lined hood framing her soft face, June Earlson leaned forward, peering across at Irina and began to talk and gesture frightenedly.

Two cars were coming uphill toward the turn ahead. Phil made jabbing motions at them and opened his window.

"Pass me!" he yelled and slowed.

Irina slowed, too, keeping abreast out there on the wrong side of the road, within fifty yards of the turn.

"What?" she yelled.

7

"PASS!"

"There's room for three cars. Get over!"

She inched her wheels closer to the Porsche's, forcing him to swerve away. June, Irina noted with satisfaction, twisted frantically around to look out at the drop-off over there on her side of the road. Phil had to abandon the idea of slowing any more because a car was coming downhill in back of him. He flashed Irina an anxious scowl. She thought gleefully that she'd sure as hell peeled off his composure fast. Finally, Irina barreled past him and dodged back into her own lane with an easy ten-foot safety margin.

For a mile or so Phil trailed her closely, watching for safe passing room. She began to decelerate down to 30—25—20 mph, forcing him to creep along behind her. When the road was clear and he started to pass, she speeded up and swung across in front of him, her tactics calculated not only to outrage him but to guarantee his full participation. Goaded enough, he wouldn't quit or let her quit. From now on, Irina knew, his involvement was with *her* instead of June.

Phil feinted, then, going to the shoulder, passed her like a rocket and the chase was on. She didn't catch him for five minutes. She passed him in a hair-raising maneuver coming off a turn. In less than a minute he took a longer risk and dropped her behind him.

It went that way, brief triumphs going back and forth from one to the other for mile after exhilarating mile of high-pitched tension. Glimpsing June in a state of near hysteria Irina laughed exultantly, and her graceful long legs, brilliantly sheathed in the red stretch pants, moved in nervous frenzy. Once when Phil tried to pass on a long straight downhill run she forced him to over 100 mph. He stayed grimly in the passing lane so long that he'd have had a head-on collision for certain if Irina hadn't slacked off and let him move in front of her.

They dropped through the foothills to the desert at a slackened pace. On the flat run to Reno, clogging traffic along the bar-and-bed line of splashy clubs and motels forced them to quit the mechanized phase of the contest.

Downtown, Phil led the way under the sign proclaiming with loud-mouthed humility, THE BIGGEST LITTLE CITY ON EARTH, and cruised past the circusy Virginia Street gambling casinos. Irina followed him into the parking lot of one of the hotels beside the river and parked three spaces to the right. The wild ride would have him overstimulated and bull-lusty for sex. Unfortunately, he had a sick girl on his hands, Irina noted, casting occasional amused glances at the other car.

With calm, feline grace and the air of unveiling an artwork, she stripped off the bizarre mask and goggles and peeled the hood back from the sleek, jet-black crown of her elegant head. The yellow parka's bulk emphasized the delicacy of her long neck, lifting like the pale stem of some exotic, haughty wildflower. The shape and balance of her small, narrow head and slender oval face had a sculptural quality, the curving lines, roundings and planes merging subtly, the ultra-feminine features honed to the exquisite edge of perfection.

The black of her hair, high-arching eyebrows and tnick lashes contrasted strikingly with the whiteness of her taut, smooth skin; the pale-pink unassertiveness of her full, soft, unpainted lips was offset by the disconcerting turquoise brilliance and challenge of her eyes.

There was a sharp flavor of dramatic clash about Irina Devereaux, a disturbing blend of repulsion and irresistible allure in her beauty. She stirred men, the unwilling as well as the rapacious, making them bold and afraid almost at the same time. Those who had felt her passion did not forget.

While Phil was unfolding himself out of his car she placed her ski boots on the ground beside her own car. Drawing her knees up, swiveling around and dropping her lower legs outside, Irina lifted herself and left the Jag in a flowing arch, pouring herself over the side into her boots. Standing with her sexy legs spread, the yellow parka fell short of her hips. Her stretch pants had crawled up and she tugged at them, jiggling her shapely knees and tilting her pelvis rapidly from side to side.

She saw that Phil was standing erect, staring across the top of the Porsche at her. She quit jiggling and, looking down at herself, began to smooth the pants. Her bare white hands moved over the clinging fiery red stretch pants lingeringly, caressing the sleek-curving, intimate contours of her luscious thighs, hips and lower body.

"Lay off!" Phil's voice was a thick, muffled shout.

She gaped in mock astonishment, flung her hands out to the sides, palms up.

9

"I didn't touch you!" she cried.

"Lay off!"

"You said that. Phil, do you know what you look like towering above that little car, glowering, and hurling wrath at me with your eyes? Jove!" she said admiringly, but added to herself, *A comic Jove.*

"I've got no desire to be Jove or any other god or anything but a normal, adjusted guy," he said. He turned militantly and walked around the car to June's door, his stride short and stiff-legged as if he were wearing leg irons. "I don't want anything to do with you, Irina."

"No?" she said tartly.

"No! Now lay off. Already you've got June sick."

"Bet I scared you gutless, too," she taunted, grinning.

"Hell!" he scoffed.

"You mean the excitement grabbed you in the guts and made you alive instead of sick?"

"If you're trying to prove something against June, forget it! I love her, and I'm going to marry her. She's my kind. I won't get involved with you, Irina."

"Baby," she said in a teasing, little-girl voice, "you're already involved. You've grabbed the high-voltage wire and can't let go."

"High-voltage you," he sneered. "Irina, the queen. Irresistible you! You really think like that, you arrogant little bitch."

"Wham . . . Wham!" She smacked her palm twice with her fist. "You won the speed event. Now the word battle. That's two for you. Best three out of five takes it, Phil. Next event, wrestling!" She laughed gleefully.

He opened his mouth, then shut it exasperatedly and yanked June's door open. He bent down tenderly and began to help her out. Irina walked over and stood with a fist on one hip, head tilted slightly to one side, her lips pushed out thoughtfully, a speculative look in her eyes as if trying to identify some odd species.

June was shaky and uncoordinated and Phil had to tug and heave her like a sack to get her upright. Then he had to hold onto her to keep her from collapsing. The round face in the cuddly, fur-lined hood looked somewhat less than cute. The eyes were glassy, the flesh doughy, the cheeks blotchy from wiped tears, the Cupid's bow mouth loose. She looked like she might vomit. Focusing on

10

Irina, June made a whimpering sound, buried her face against Phil and clung to him.

Phil glared at Irina, who offered: "I'll help you upstairs with her."

June cried out protestingly.

"Irina, go away," Phil growled, "Keep away from the suite, too. Understand?"

"I'm afraid I do," Irina said solemnly, though her bright eyes sparkled with amusement. "And you should be ashamed. A sick girl. A defenseless girl. After all, Phil! . . . Juney dear, don't you worry. I won't let him get you alone."

June wailed, "Make her go away."

"You heard her, Irina. And don't go near that suite."

Irina's humor vanished. The idea of his giving his strength to that creature became unbearable. The sight of them bound together to shut her out made her raw with anger. Her voice razor-slashed.

"Try to keep me out! I paid my share. I'll use it when I please. I *please* right now!"

She spun and started away. Then as Phil got June moving sluggishly, she stopped to fasten the top buckle of each ski boot. She used the Porsche as a footstool and Phil saw red—specifically, the seat of her stretch pants. A second later she made him see red again—the backs of her fleet, swinging legs moving away.

She entered the hotel and crossed the casino. Rebuffing the smiles and glances of the sparse crowd with an expression of cool hauteur she zigzagged around a roulette wheel, black jack deal tables and slot machine and entered a waiting elevator in the lobby.

"Four," she told the operator.

Key in hand she hurried down the fourth-floor corridor to 405 and unlocked it. She went in, flipping the wall switch to light the several lamps of a sitting room with false fireplace, mantel, easy chairs and two sofas. There was a connected bedroom on each side, one for the five men in the party, another for the six girls. She left the hall door wide-open and went into the girls' bedroom, passing between two pairs of pushed-together twin beds that looked neat and semivirginal under their pink spreads. Shrugging out of her parka and going to the double bed in the corner where, ironically, she slept with the party's only authentic virgin, Irina sat briefly on the edge of the bed and unbuckled her ski boots. She got them off by standing up and kicking sharply.

The jingle fragment of a song written by a campus clown ran through her mind: *Irina . . . Irina . . . Oh, you gorgeous queen-a . . . why must you be so mean-a?* She remembered the look of "the lovers" shutting her out and she had to fight an abrupt impulse to slam, lock and chain-lock every door and make them plead to get into the suite.

She controlled herself, but the violent emotion gave the exquisitely honed beauty of her face a look of sultry passion. Her mouth compressed, and her eyelids were drawn so close together that the thick black lashes seemed to hover like smoke, veiling the color, but not the intensity, of her eyes.

Irina is in command here! she thought, and returned to the sitting room, moving on tiptoe. She was aware of the clean-lined elegance of her lithe young body in stretch pants and a matching sweater that clung to the lifting points of her breasts, individually defined and jiggling prettily. The lust-inciting power of her figure she knew quite well. She stationed herself in the doorway and waited.

The romantic team got off the elevator and came down the corridor looking like an ambulance detail with a casualty. Phil plodded along in a stooped (spelled "stupid") position, holding up the sad sack. June, as her kind always did, was playing the pitiful role to the hilt, using her weakness as a bludgeon. A boomerang-shaped bludgeon! Irina grinned tartly. She cautioned herself not to get smug, but to use her imagination. In June's position she'd bring up reinforcements at this stage of the battle. Probably a doctor.

"I'm going to phone for a doctor," Irina said.

"I don't want a doctor," June whined. "I just want to lie down a while."

"I insist on a doctor."

"*You* insist," June cried. "Phil, if she thinks she can boss me around . . . "

"She can't," Phil assured her. "You're blocking the doorway. Let us through."

"Sure." She stepped aside.

She shut the door behind them and followed closely

into the bedroom. At the nearest bed June let her shaky knees buckle and sat in a heap. Phil helped her out of the fur-hooded coat, showing her in a bulky sweater and baggy corduroy pants tucked into heavy galoshes. Irina stood by and watched June lie on her back, sighing and closing her eyes.

"She going to die with her boots on?"

"I'm tending to that," Phil snapped and sat at the foot of the bed. While he worked with the galoshes, Irina pulled off his black knitted cap and walked her fingers through his blond hair. He ducked, twisting his head to look at her from the corner of his eye. Irina winked and grinned, touching her upper lip with the tip of her tongue. She ran her forefinger down the sensitive back of his neck. Involuntarily Phil smiled, then immediately frowned.

"Keep your hands off him!" June raised herself on her elbows, squinching up her round little face.

"Don't you have to go to the bathroom?" Irina said.

"No, I don't! Of all the gall—deliberately bringing up something unattractive like that!"

"I just asked."

"You just asked!" June mimicked bitterly, then groaned: "Oh-h-h!" and flopped back, inert.

"Now look what you've done!" Phil moved up the bed and petted June's face. He looked at Irina reproachfully. "I thought you had more decency than to pick on somebody that's down."

"I throw in the towel," Irina said heatedly, flinging out her hands. "I won't play her kind of game, making myself weak and dependent to give a man an exaggerated notion of his strength. I want the true strength of a man. I don't happen to be fixated at the child level that seems to appeal to you so much. I'm a woman and proud of it and I want a man who's glad I am and doesn't need any fake ego props to convince him he's man enough, because he knows it already."

"Darling," June warned, "she's trying to goad you into proving something you don't need to prove."

"Now that you've figured it out for me," he said sarcastically, "I get it. I couldn't appreciate it more if I was one of the first-grade pupils you've been doing your practice teaching on."

13

"You're too kind to *want* to hurt me," June said for-
givingly. "*She's* doing this to you."

"Oh, she is, is she? You mean I'm some kind of dummy,
not responsible for what it says?"

"I didn't mean it that way."

"That's how it came out."

"Now you're picking on me."

"I'm sorry."

"You should be."

"Aspirins help. Let me get you some," he offered.

"No."

"Maybe a little drink'll relax you."

"No."

"Well, do you *want* to suffer?"

"I refuse to quarrel." June put a forearm across her
eyes and lay silent.

"But, darling—"

"I refuse to quarrel."

It was in a tone of moral superiority that she issued
what amounted to an order to shut his mouth. Phil
obeyed, but not without resentment. Irina noted the
lumping of his clenched jaw muscle just below his ear
lobe, and the urge to say four words made her tongue
tingle. She said nothing, knowing it was more effective to
let him *feel* "the tyranny of weakness" June was imposing
and always had imposed on him.

Let him ponder the guilts and frustrations of a future
filled with whinings, snivelings and martyred reproaches.
Then, as a prisoner looks at freedom, he would look at
her, Irina, and the untamed male instinct she'd already
roused would flare rebelliously and rip through his self-
control.

She shifted her weight, drawing his eye to her enticingly bent knee. He looked at her legs, then abruptly at
her face.

"I can't throw you out, Irina," he said in a low, hard
voice, "but I can ask you in a civilized way to let the kid
sleep."

"I'll be quiet," she said, her voice and eyes and smile
so soft he couldn't look at her. "If you'd rather, I'll go in
the sitting room."

"I'd rather."

"You come, too."

"Don't you dare go with her!" June, coming eye-poppingly alive, seized Phil's hand.

"Calm down. I'm not going."

Irina turned up a palm, then drifted over to the big double bed with a lazy, swaying grace, her hips rolling faintly. She lowered herself onto one knee on the bed, doubling the leg under, the other extended back full length, giving Phil one of his favorite profile views of her. She pulled and tugged the spread free, tossed it casually onto another bed, then turned the covers down nearly to the foot of the bed. She sat on the edge of the white sheet half-facing Phil and June, both suspiciously watchful, and lifting her arms, began to unpin her hair in back.

When she freed her hair it fell almost to her shoulders, and she stirred it out loosely around her cheeks, its darkness touching her pale face with intimate shadows. The wanton effect needed no seductive looks to go with it. In fact, she remained expressionless as if alone and involved with routine. She stretched her arms overhead and seemed about to yawn and hit the sack.

They weren't expecting it when she stood up and casually began to take off her stretch pants. Carrying the panties underneath with them, she peeled them down from the narrow incurve of her waist, baring the smooth, soft-curved flare of her hips, upper buttocks and several inches of her belly below the navel. The expanding nakedness, shocking white within the opening red frame, drew a piercing yell from June.

"Stop it . . . Stop it . . . You stop doing that."

"If you don't like it," Irina said equably, continuing to strip the pants down, "don't look."

June rolled away, buried her face in the pillow and had a tantrum, kicking her feet. Phil was already up and charging, his face red, his gaze riveted to her bare flesh, when she pushed the pants and panties down below her hips. His outspread hands aimed themselves at her moving hands and she felt a burst of fiery joy so intense she laughed aloud and literally hopped up and down.

"Sharkan," she cried gleefully.

They both knew the Arabian Nights tale of the match between Sharkan, the undefeated, mightiest wrestler, and Queen Abrise. The feel of the soft frail body of the beautiful young queen took all the fight out of Sharkan.

15

"Careful, Sharkan!"

Phil caught her hands and the top of the pants and began trying to pull them up. She got her hands free and wound her arms up around his neck and pulled him off balance onto the bed on top of her.

She tried to kiss him, but he turned his face and grimly tugged at the pants, hauling them up and up, and his fingers didn't linger to caress, but presently she could feel that he was sexually roused. When he tried to draw away, she entwined her legs with his and pushed her lower body hard against him and hung onto his head. He glared down into her face and she gazed softly up at him, her startling, wildflower eyes wide-open. She pushed her lips out to be kissed.

"Please, Phil," she whispered, "Kiss me, dearest."

Abruptly he fastened his lips to hers and bore down hard, rolling his head from side to side. His hands beneath her fitted themselves possessively to her flesh and after a moment he thrust his tongue deep into her mouth. He was fire-hot and began to move his body in a wavelike rhythm on top of her. But June was there, shrilling and pulling hysterically at his belt and hitting him.

"Stop it, Phil! . . . Phil! . . . *Phil,* come to your senses!"

She got through to him. Phil broke the kiss. Panting a little, a groggy expression on his face, he looked back across his shoulder and began to nod. He gave Irina a pained, craving look and pulled himself free and got off the bed. He walked nervously across the room. June paced him, jabbering, her voice breaking in little half-sobs.

Irina lay throbbing on her back, her breath and heartbeat quick. Waves of sexual desire flooded her body. She stretched her legs, arching her feet tensely. She locked her ankles, knees and thighs together, trying to hold tight. The rushing heat in her flesh made every restraint unbearable.

She rolled forward into a sitting position and seizing her sweater with crossed hands ripped it off over her head and flung it to the floor. There was a frail vulnerability about the slightness of her bare upper body and narrow, sloping shoulders when she took off her bra. She drew a deep breath that tautened the sleek curve line of her back and her nakedly beautiful breasts were raised, their white

16

cones richly tipped by dark red, circular aureoles and stiffened nipples.

She lay back and, bracing her feet and lifting her body, got the stretch pants and panties down to her knees in a kind of frenzy. In another few seconds they were off completely and she lay naked, one knee up, and gazed at Phil. June rushed out into the sitting room and slammed the door.

Phil, torn, looked at the door, then at Irina. He wiped his head. She lay gazing at him and reached out a hand toward him.

"Come here.'"

"I can't!" He drew a long breath and reached for the doorknob. "I've got to go to her." He opened the door, started through.

"I'll be in the shower when you come back!" she called urgently. "I've got to have you. I need you, Phil . . . You need me. . . ."

When he left she ran to the bathroom.

She was finishing in the shower when he opened the stall door. He stepped in stark naked and clasped her slick, wet, shiny body to him and kissed her repeatedly on the mouth, his hands moving over her in gliding caresses. Then a kind of spasm ran through him and he clutched her bottom and mashed her to him forcibly.

The hot, thrusting feel of his demanding naked maleness against her body made her squirm. She twisted and tried to pull away, but he imprisoned her, his face grim, his body mindless with passion. He lifted her off her feet, holding her under her upper thighs and slid himself between her knees and pressed her back into a corner.

"Please, Phil," she begged. "No . . . Not yet . . . Not here, Phil . . . Let me down."

"No."

She slapped him hard, once. The second slap was harder. He shook his head and let her down. She scurried out of the stall, caught up a towel and threw it at him.

"Dry me. Hurry."

He grinned delightedly and positioned himself in front of her.

"I see you remember how," she said.

He nodded happily and dried her hands. She then extended her arms, rested her fingertips on his wide, muscular shoulders and smiled obscurely up into his face as

17

he dried her arms and carefully blotted her face and throat.

She kept her fingertips on his shoulders while he worked the towel down the front and sides of her body. And where at first she had had to reach up, she was soon reaching down. He had begun six feet tall as against her five foot three, and he ended less than half her height as he crouched, attending her feet. She turned herself and as he worked his way up her back, she smiled across her shoulder, watching the rippling play of those powerful arm and shoulder muscles serving her.

"Love me, Phil? Sorry you were so mean?"

"Yes."

"Show me."

She swung a little to one side, brushing his cheek with the cheek of her compact, round bottom. He kissed her there.

"What am I?" she prompted.

"Delicious . . . adorable . . . irresistible . . . "

Embracing her hips and turning her in a complete circle he kissed her all the way around. She stood smiling, reaching down to tousle his hair.

"That's enough, lover."

He swiftly finished the toweling and she pulled off her shower cap, tossed it in the washbasin, and shook out her hair. Phil caught her up in his arms and carried her into the bedroom, which was dark, the door to the sitting room shut.

"You lock the door?" she whispered.

"Yes."

He sat her on the bed and placed the two pillows atop each other in the center. He lifted her onto them, settling her hips comfortably, her pelvis tilted up. He felt her from the tips of her toes to her breasts and kissed her nipples and belly.

He came forward between her legs, standing on his knees, and she could see the powerful bulk of him, silhouetted darkly there above her. He came into intimate contact with her and she felt a shiver in his flesh and a serge of sensation in her genitals. And then he was entering her slowly, withdrawing partially, moving deeper, withdrawing again.

Abruptly he seized her hips and thrust himself fully. She had the glorious sense of bringing him down from his

18

height and of commanding every last ounce of his power and will and mind. She began to move herself in a furious, violent rhythm, forcing his pace and making him cling to her. Love words and kisses poured worshipfully from him and then, together they raced to the feverish heights of ecstasy.

When they were at last sated with each other, their energies spent, she pushed him away from her and reached out in the dark for the phone.

"Who are you calling, darling?" he said indifferently.

"Sky Hi Ski Lodge," she said into the phone. She reached her free hand to Phil, pressed her palm to his lips. He was still kissing it when she got the Lodge and had Jim Carthage paged.

"What's with Jim, Irina?" Phil raised himself on one elbow. She hooked his head in her arm, pulled his face to her breast.

"Jim's holding the stakes," she began. "Jim? Irina. It's done. I won the bet. Get on down here; I'll buy the drinks for the party."

She hung up. Phil lifted his face from her naked breast.

"What the hell! You did this to win a bet?"

She reached down his body, touching him seductively.

"Un-huh." She stroked him. "You give a damn?"

"Damn right I give a damn!"

"Relax," she purred, continuing to caress him. He pushed her hand away but it crept back.

"Just to win a bet—stop it, Irina!—just to win a bet you deliberately almost wrecked us on the road and deliberately bitched June up and made me do this to her. You're lying there and admitting it?"

"Yes."

Despite his anger he was rousing sexually.

"Not just admitting, but bragging—Irina, if you don't quit that I'll hurt you!"

"Don't fight it, lover," she whispered, increasing the erotic stimulation, and he didn't have the will to stop her.

He began to curse her, then had to take a breath. He finished lamely, "I never really knew what a bitch you are."

She didn't answer, just lay there insidiously reconquering and taming him. As the pitch of his desire heightened, the protest left his lips, and silenced, they came begging for the touch of hers. She turned her face away.

19

"You called me a bitch."

"Darling, forgive me." He kissed her throat and pleaded: "I want you . . . I want you. . . ."

"You can blame me for the first time you betrayed her. If you do it now, after I've leveled with you, how're you going to squirm out of the responsibility?"

"Don't tease me. I can't stand it. I've got to have you."

She allowed him to come into position. At the last instant, just when he imagined he was going to get his satisfaction, she scooted back away from him and in a rolling whipping motion, leaped off the bed. Evading his clumsy grab and laughing softly, she streaked into the bathroom and locked the door.

chapter two

The gang trooped in high-spiritedly a half-hour later, looking robust in their ski outfits, and sounding as if they'd spent their time at the Lodge floating the dinner steaks on toddies. Irina, in a fresh, princess-cut dress of silver-gray satin and narrow, high-heeled black pumps, stood in front of the mock fireplace presiding over a pair of carts stocked with liquors, mixers, glasses and ice.

"Come and get it," she sang out gaily. "It's ready and waiting. A Rocky Scotch for you, Jim, y'ole swivel-hip slaloming Doubting Thomas . . . and for your better-half Esther, gin 'n' ginger ale. . . . A Seventy-seven for Nick, girl watcher *magna cum laude* and for Diane doll, your favorite watchee (next to me, natch), bourbon and side of Coke . . . . bourbon highball for Pete; the same, milder, for your sweetie and my bedmate Linda. And for John and Jon—maybe I should say Comrades —suspicious vodkas mixed with *red* tomato juice . . . "

Chattering and handing out the drinks while they laughed and joked with her, Irina ignored their good-natured prodding for details and proof of her conquest. June was hiding out in the bedroom. Phil, in slacks and sport shirt, hung around the edge of things, the expression on his face vaguely neutral, like an unsmiled smile. Irina poured a double bourbon in a tumbler, tore open a tiny packet of salt, and pointed dramatically across the room at him.

"Last, and maybe not least, I have for Phil Harkness a double bourbon with a lick of salt to keep it down. Come and get it, Phil. No time to be shy."

When he didn't move she clapped her hands. "Jim . . . Nick . . . deliver him!"

Grinning, they walked militantly over, took him by the arms and marched him to her. The girls were bright-eyed, the men laughing and leering.

"Now, Phil," Jim said. "Eighteen dollars is riding on this thing. Does Irina the queen-a take it? Or will you lie like a good buddy?"

"Ho!" Irina said. She took a hotel envelope from her skirt pocket and lied glibly: "I took the precaution of gathering evidence. Seventeen chest hairs. I guess you didn't notice when I plucked 'em."

He blinked so comically that everybody roared with laughter. After a moment he laughed with them.

"Pay the devil her due," Phil said. Sighing, Jim slapped the cash into Irina's hand.

"Feeling no pain at the time, eh, Phil?" John laughed. Nick offered mock sympathy. "How you must have suffered!" Pete sniffed and wiped at his eye. "Poor Phil. Beaten. Would that I could've borne this defeat for you!"

"Say!" Pete's fiancé, Linda, a strapping, handsome, red-faced girl, elbowed him sharply. "Where d'ya get that would you could've been in his place?"

"I said that? Oh, Lord!" He caught her in his arms. "It means it's happening, I'm losing my mind." He kissed her mouth twice. "Save me . . . save me. . . Unlock thy steel pants, O, Flower of the Occident."

Linda pushed him away. She gave Irina a fawning smile and raised her glass.

"Here's to you, Irina," she said and drank. "You sure give me a kick. It doesn't matter how different our viewpoints are, I can't help liking you."

"That goes double," Irina said sweetly, her smile obscuring the contempt in her eyes.

She knew Linda hated her, and though the Amazon was physically capable of breaking her in pieces, the disgusting worm had been appeasing her with lavish compliments and little services ever since they'd come on the party. She even kissed her at bedtime, then hardly

21

dared sleep for fear Irina might sneak off to Pete. Far from reassuring her, Irina subtly pointed out that the only sure way to match her challenge was to give up her precious virginity.

"I don't blame you for a minute," Linda said soothingly. "Phil was yours before that June ever came along. You just took back what she'd stolen from you."

"To the victor belongs even the virtue," Irina said wryly.

"What'd you say, honey?" Linda cupped her ear.

Somebody had turned on both radio and TV. One couple was dancing, others were shouting and laughing noisily. Irina poured a shot of bourbon, tossed it off straight.

"I say," she laughed, "I know you're happy it was *June's* man I took."

"Oh, I can't hear a thing. I'm going in and put on my party dress."

Within the hour everyone had changed clothes and drunk too much and there was a fine, high-swinging mood of hilarity. Hailing Irina as a *femme fatale,* they smacked their lips and cornered her in pairs and groups, demanding details and she handed out tidbits in a way that made them whoop. They called Phil dog and devil and lover boy admiringly. He was at first sheepishly unsure about the gang's attitude, but catching their mood of approval he basked and strutted like a hero. He even danced with her.

"Flying, Phil?" Irina shouted.

"Flying!"

Pete cut in. Then John. She danced and flirted with all the men, letting them build up a little steam—in Jim's case a little too much. He practically dragged Esther into the men's bedroom and locked the door. Everybody cheered them. Except June. She'd changed into a pink and white frock and ventured out timidly, her face long and miserable.

Somebody got her a drink and several of them surrounded her, laughing and coaxing her into seeing it all as a big, jazzy joke, a lusty-young-fun thing, nothing to gloom about. She got the drink down and the corners of her mouth up in a strained smile. She threatened to sink the whole party.

Irina clapped her hands and shouted. "I propose a

22

toast to the best sport in the whole damned gang, Miss June Earlson!"

"Hey, hey! I'll drink to that!"

"Here's to June! Bottoms up, everybody!"

"Let's give this some college spirit. How's about the old locomotive?" Nick yelled, and led them all in a "J-U-N-E E-A-R-L-S-O-N . . . June Earlson, June Earlson, June Earlson . . . HOORAY!"

Jim and Esther came out and got in on the tail end, then somebody suggested they sing the college song, and they gathered round and rendered it with feeling that got so maudlin on the final note that Irina had to pick up her mood again.

"Now for a dance," she proposed. "A solo. Phil and June." She started to applaud and the others joined in like an ape chorus, she thought derisively.

They danced to cheers, and Irina went over and got herself another drink and answered the phone and assured the management they'd quiet down immediately. A half-hour later things were so full blast, the manager came up in person.

"We'll all be good," Irina promised, "and we'll all kiss you," she said, giving him a long kiss on the mouth that made him blush and rush off.

Meantime John and Jon had sessioned in the men's bedroom and Nick and Diane went in for their turn. Irina pouted and sat on Pete's lap.

"Nobody wants to be alone with Irina," she said, her voice slurred. "Nobody loves Irina."

"*I* love Irina," Pete declared.

"You don't."

"No. No. I do!"

"But you're Linda's."

"She's half-passed out. Lookit 'er," he said, nodding at the other sofa where she was sprawled in a corner.

"Love her. When Nick 'n' Diane come out, take her in there."

"She wouldn't let me."

"Pete, you gotta so she'll lay off me. She kisses me in bed. Look how she's awake now and jealous 'cause you're hugging me."

Phil came and wanted to dance and she got off Pete's lap. She lost track of time and June. Then she saw June standing like a dejected ghost in the girls' bedroom, peer-

23

ing in at the party with a woebegone expression. Irina turned away angrily, got herself another drink.

She didn't know how much later she felt a kind of shadow beginning to creep over the party. Two of the girls stood talking earnestly together and looking at the girls' bedroom door intently. It was closed. Everyone began to notice.

"What's up?" Nick called happily, coming out of the men's side with Diane. "Where's the drinks? What's the slow-down? This a party or study group?"

"June's awful unhappy," Esther said worriedly.

"Ah, what the hell! Tell her to be a sport and forget it," Jim said.

But he looked anxiously at the shut door, too.

"She wouldn't be crazy enough to do anything screwy, would she?"

There was a sudden, total silence. Everybody looked at each other uncertainly. Phil strode hastily to the door, turned the knob.

"It's locked!" He began to bang his fist on the panel. "June!" he shouted. "June, are you all right? June! Open up! Isn't there a key to this door? Somebody try the hall door."

There was a flurry of activity. A key was found. The door opened to the end of the chain lock.

They shouted June's name but got no answer. Someone ran into the hall.

"What if she's killed herself?" Linda said, color draining from her big, red face. "What if that's what Irina Devereaux did to that poor girl?"

"Don't get hysterical," Irina said icily.

They got the hall door unlocked and went in.

June was on the bathroom floor, bleeding from the wrists.

"Omigod, omigod," Phil moaned, sinking to his knees. He lifted her to a sitting position. "Somebody tear a rag or gimme a tie or belt for a tourniquet."

"Hold her arms straight up. There's not much bleeding."

The next half-hour was frantic and sickly sobering.

June came to, weakly. From the amount of blood on the floor it was judged she hadn't lost much. It was decided not to call a doctor; there might be a scandal, expulsions from school.

24

They got June comfortably to bed and then most of them sat dully out in the sitting room, looking at each other from opposite sofas. They avoided looking at Irina. She took it as long as she could, then spoke.

"One thing about martyrs, they don't figure to be dead and miss out on hearing the applause. She made nice shallow cuts in a nice safe place where we'd be sure to find her and save her. Well, I'm not going to sit around through a wake for the undead. I'm heading back to San Francisco right now. Who'll help me with my luggage —Pete?"

"Sure thing, Irina," he said, hopping up.

Phil stared at her bleakly from the doorway.

"You dare make a cold-blooded speech like that when it was all your fault!"

"I dare, yes." She rushed at him, stood facing him, fists on hips. "You dare to judge me, do you? Well, who made vows of loyalty to her, you or me? Who broke 'em, you or me? Am I big enough to rape you? Admit you're a weak slob! I'll admit it for you! You not only wanted me once, but after I told you I did it on a bet you tried to make love to me again! And you were ashamed of yourself. But—" she made a sweeping gesture—"all of *them* decided it was a big joke so *you* trotted along with their opinion and laughed it up big. That's how *characterless* you are! And that's exactly why I dumped you. Pete, are you getting my luggage?"

"Coming right up, Irina."

Minutes later in the parking lot, her luggage stowed in the Jag, she said, "You're riding with Jim, aren't you? He was going to bring down my skis and poles. Will you see he doesn't forget to bring them?"

"Sure. Do I get a kiss for the services?"

"I'm too mad and disgusted with everybody. As if I'm all to blame for everything."

"Hell, you told Phil the truth. Nobody raped him."

"Thanks, Pete." She gripped his hand, smiled affectionately. "Still and all I was a heel. I'm kind of sorry for the girl. I ought to pick on somebody my size, I guess. I . . . I wish I hadn't done it."

"I'm glad to hear you say that, Irina."

"Pete, I like you."

"I really go for you, Irina. I don't know how I got into

this deal with Linda. A party mood or something. I don't know how to break it up."

"Pete, what I said about her making les moves at me —that was a damned lie," she said contritely.

"I didn't take it seriously."

"And I oughtn't to've egged you on to seduce her. For all I know, she couldn't take it, psychologically."

"That's so with her. She was brought up that way. She'd think afterward that she'd become a lost soul. She couldn't cope with it. But, I tell you, Irina, I just can't stand it, sometimes. I'm scrambling for dough to get through school, so I can't even think about marriage. So where am I?"

"You want to be with me real bad, Pete?"

"Hell, yes, Irina!"

"Then, okay. Get your gear and drive back with me now."

"Bay-bee!" he exclaimed. "Oh-oh, here comes trouble."

It was Linda, striding furiously out of the hotel.

"What're you doing down here, Pete? I want to know what you're doing down here so long. I want to know if you want your ring back. I want to know this minute!"

She came to a stop, paces away, her eyes stark, her mouth trembling.

"I want to know," she cried.

Irina started the Jag.

"Make up your mind, Pete," she told him.

"Wait," he said.

"Make up your mind, Pete," Linda parroted Irina.

"Well . . . " He said nervously.

Linda began to swallow rapidly and blink her eyes.

"Don't blink the tears back. Let 'em roll," Irina called. "No matter if she hasn't got anything else, a gal's always got tears of self-pity to work for her. Well, Pete, you're wavering, so bye-bye. . . . After all, Irina can't win 'em all."

She backed, then sent the car forward in a roaring arc out into the street.

She was free and on the move with an invigorating wind washing coldly over her face and blowing her skirt above the tops of her nylons. She fought the skirt for a while, then shrugged. A traffic light stopped her beside a trailer truck, and the driver stared down at her naked thighs.

"If you can't see well enough, I'll brighten my dash lights."

"That'd help."

She laughed and when the light changed she thumbed her nose and sped off.

Within seconds she'd dropped him back into what she thought of as the dead zone of used-up time-space known as the past. The brief, already forgotten experience became part of the past, equal in unimportance with all the rest of it.

She focused on the now of desert and stars and white-capped mountains like ghost gods ahead and the synchronized action of the Jaguar's engine, a thrilling dazzle of motion stripped of emotion. She visualized the ballet of turning shafts, spinning cams, gleaming steel-on-steel thrust of pistons into cylinders. Now, as often, she fancied the car as rescuer, knight in armor and embracing lover, responding to the burning fuel heat she provided with vibrations that penetrated her flesh.

In a way the Jaguar, which she had bought with *his* permission, was like *him*: separate from her, it waited, unalive; at her whim it stirred; when she so desired, it throbbed; if she willed it, it would roar forth, past every obstacle.

She accelerated till the sound was deafening. But the noise would not drown two silences: June's, when, wearing her prettiest pink and white dress, her hair fluffy, her mouth brightly painted, she'd stood looking in at the party, rejected even though she'd done her best to be pleasing—and Linda's as she had waited, mouth trembling, eyes blinking back tears.

Irina felt a stinging in the corners of her eyes. There was a heaviness in her chest and she began to massage the slow-growing lump in her throat.

"Hell!" she said angrily. "To hell with it."

But the pain and sadness persisted, threatening to engulf her. *Their* pain, *their* sadness. To hell with them if they couldn't protect themselves. *Get tough, sisters, get tough!* she thought grittily. Her eyes felt raw. She had a furious impulse to turn back and take Pete after all. It wasn't true she couldn't win 'em all. She could. But she didn't want Pete any more than she'd wanted Phil. They had no meaning.

27

The only man who ever had had a meaning, the only one she had ever wanted, was . . . she didn't dare even think his name. Just as she'd put a continent between them, she had willed him out of her thoughts. But he was never gone. Always his essence was there, vital within her, like the very tissue of her heart. Wherever he was, he loved her. Wherever she was, she loved him. Whatever gratifications he found in others were substitutes. Whatever gratifications she found were substitutes.

She clenched her teeth. What had happened to boldness, aggression, assertion in men? Those heroic qualities frightened this tame society. Heroes of the past with protest in their guts would today be the pariahs, the criminals, the insane. Even *he* was afraid to flout convention, afraid to face the truth, to make his own law and claim what was his.

She slowed the car and began to "drive scared." Risk for its own sake was empty; recklessness was a form of fear, an evasion of the real thing.

The time had come, Irina resolved, the time had come —she drew a long breath—to face the truth. To live the truth. To force the issue and *make* Larry, *Larry,* LARRY claim her!

No matter, no matter—she let her breath out slowly —that Larry was her mother's husband.

chapter three

It was still night as she rode the great waves of land down out of the mountains, swallowing every few miles to clear her ears. But on the East Coast dawn was breaking. Pearl gray, pink, then golden light was flowing silently across Larry's land, streams, pond, woods and splendid hilltop house and creeping into the master bedroom where Larry and her mother slept separately in enormous custom-made beds.

Her mother, for all the dynamic qualities of her waking personality, returned nightly to the womb. Lying motionless on her side in a fetal curl, ear plugs and eye mask shutting out the world, she was insignificant in the bed's expanse.

Larry, unless he'd spent the night in his New York apartment, would be stretched out in all directions in masterful possession of the other bed, his leonine head, broad handsome face, strong body and long limbs magnificent.

Irina imagined him moving very slowly but constantly from one position to another, because the force lighting his deep brown eyes with eloquence, driving his brilliant mind and achieving his daylight goals, was sleepless, restless. It pressed relentlessly like some profound, dark tide toward the hidden, forbidden, unachieved goals.

She drove across the Central Valley toward Sacramento, her eyes glittery, as she wondered mystically if her thoughts had reached him, if he was aware of the imminence of her long-distance phone call. The mysticism made her uneasy. She shook her head. No, he wasn't aware, but if he were . . . she could just see the smile on his sleeping face.

Not that she had ever actually seen him in bed—except once eight years ago when she was fourteen, just a few months after Larry had become her father.

One night she woke sharply, feeling out of breath, her heart beating so fast it scared her. She switched on the lamp and jumped out of bed. With a panicky sense of unreality she saw herself in three places at once. Maybe she existed only on the glass surfaces of the dresser mirror, on the full-length bathroom door mirror, and on the panes of the French door to her little balcony. The door's crisscrossing wooden strips were like guidelines for a child's drawing.

The figure in a shorty nightgown was all arms and legs stretching out of a bodiless puff of smoke. But it was all too real, including that tone of overalertness as though something within her were always nervously poised for flight, or fight.

There was no denying the skimpy neck or uncurlable frenzy of black hair or eyes staring like white glass balls with the color painted on. Or that strained, anxious face with its range of moods and mercurial changes of expression from sweetness to savagery, beauty to ugliness.

29

She was her mother's image, her miniature, and Irina knew from snapshot albums at her grandparents' that year by year throughout childhood she was her duplicate.

Nevertheless, no matter how hard she tried, her mother always rejected her and loved her other children more and noticed nothing but the bad things she did and didn't understand her and wasn't proud of her and wanted her dead and made her feel unreal. *That,* she knew, was why she felt unreal, when physically she was real. Because she had only been *imagining* that Larry existed. Suddenly, she *had* to know if he was really there.

She hurried to the door, stopped. She looked down at her bareness in the skimpy nightgown, automatically raised her hand to bite her fingernails, instantly stopped herself. She stood moving her feet up and down, hesitantly. She didn't feel sexy, but too many people thought she was, and even if she wasn't lovable she was desirable.

From the time she was five and that solemn, proper governess had started doing those secret things to her she'd had a knowledge of the power of sex and of hypocrisy. She'd learned even more about those things from a grown uncle when she was eleven. And both he and that hypocrite governess had accused her of seducing them.

Now that she had prettier legs and more hips and little breasts, even people with no sly intentions liked looking at her. She rushed to the closet and covered herself from throat to instep in a bulky robe. She musn't be the slightest temptation to Larry, if he was real.

At the last instant before going into the hall she dropped the robe. Because if his seemingly genuine, clean love was just a front, she wanted to know—the quicker, the better. Going down to the second floor she scowled. She stood outside the dimly lit sky-blue door to the master bedroom, feeling chilly, afraid to turn the knob, but turning it. She eased the door open and looked in at him and her mother in the large beds. Then she tiptoed across and stood trembling at the edge of Larry's bed.

One of his outflung hands lay there and she steadied her fingers and touched it. The pads of her fingertips rested light as breath on the rounds of his knuckles, and a shiver went up her arm and through her new breasts and down her thin body. At her touch his hand rolled over and, forming a loose fist, embraced hers. She dropped to her knees and they peered through the shadows into each other's eyes. And his other hand came out and caressed her forehead and temple very slowly, very soothingly, and her heart ached.

"What's wrong?" he whispered.

"Larry," she whispered, "am I really what you said?"

"You mean are you my favorite?"

"Yes. It's not that I don't want you to love my brother and sister, too, but . . ." her voice choked up, "you haven't changed your mind, have you?"

"Of course not, Irina."

"I'll live up to it, I promise."

"I know you will, dear. But you shouldn't be here now."

She kissed his hand, stood up and, instantly obedient, hurried back to her own room. She lay awake for a long time in a serene state of exaltation, pressing to her breast the hand that hand nestled in his warm fist, her other hand retracing the area of her forehead and temple and hair which he had touched with such understanding, protective love.

Never again would she say or think that Noel Devereaux, her two-year-older brother, belonged to his mother and Elaine Devereaux, her year-younger sister, belonged to her father and Irina Devereaux belonged only to Irina Devereaux. Now she belonged to Larry and she was precious and beautiful and sweet and clean and repentant.

She couldn't wait for daylight so she could go and hug and kiss her pretty-doll baby sister. Oh, how she'd loved Elly when she was a darling fat-cheeked toddler. Elly had followed her everywhere with those sweet, trustful eyes, knowing that her Irina would protect her. Irina began to cry remembering the frightening, abusive things she'd done to Elaine later.

And poor Noel! When he was five and she was three a boy at a playground threw sand on her and made her cry and Noel yelled at the boy and hit him and then came and petted her and cried, too, because he was so full of sympathy and love.

Oh, she sobbed into her pillow, how could she have turned on Noel and fought him dirty and got him punished the way she had? Instead of being a good sister to him she'd become a bad enemy and he flinched away from any clash with her—or with anybody else. She

31

would beg his forgiveness and never call him a sissy mama's boy. Instead she'd tell him how handsome and manly he was and that he mustn't be scared of Larry. She would see to it that he started feeling at home and safe.

Most important, she'd go to her mother and announce that she had changed. She'd resolve, vow and promise never to distress her again by flightiness, defiance, scornful remarks, bad manners, untidiness, sulks, or expulsions from schools. Except her mother might cut her to ribbons in that easy, casual, unbeatable way of hers. Maybe saying drily all in one sentence: "If virtue's the order of the day, you must've topped yourself, so comb your hair and change your dress, it's lunchtime."

Or she might turn on one of those smiles that made her so devastatingly beautiful you couldn't hate her and say sweetly: "Why be so intense, Irina, as if you have to convince me? Don't I always believe you?" As if because she'd happened to fail in the past, her intentions hadn't been sincere. Worst, if she just gave her one of those silent, weary looks, she'd go all to pieces. She'd want to scream like she had when she was four or five: "I love you hardest of everybody." Meaning harder than Noel, whom she was always petting and praising, did, harder than Elaine, who she thought was prettiest, did.

In those days she'd fought so passionately for total possession of her mother that when Noel was taken onto her lap first it hurt her like scalding water. When it came her turn she'd run away yelling, "Make me!" Other times she'd yell, "You're ugly," when she meant "beautiful."

Even when she got in frenzies, hitting her mother's legs with her fists and butting and trying to bite and wanting to hurt her and knock her down, it was so she could kiss her so much she wouldn't want to get away and belong to anybody else.

At fourteen that five-year-old wildness seemed fantastic. The fact that her mother was possessed by Larry overjoyed her. He practically worshiped her and her mother was very happy, and Irina was happy for her. The love between herself and Larry was special. Not that it was superior to the more complete relationship he had with her mother; it was simply of a different nature. It was fulfilled merely by existing—asking nothing, giving everything, bringing out the finest in each of them. Now, at

32

twenty-two that fourteen-year-old—and fifteen-, sixteen- and seventeen-year-old—tameness seemed fantastic.

Passing through a sleeping Sacramento, she knew Larry would be sitting up. There'd be a rap on the hall door and whichever of the maids was in the cook's good graces would have the privilege of seeing him in his pajamas and proferring his morning coffee tray. He'd take it to the shower, where he'd have his first cup and a cigarette while the cool water flowed over his clean, tanned shoulders and deep chest and flat-muscled, fist-proof belly and rock-hard legs.

The thought of him undressed made her giddy. But just as her eyes shied away in actuality from the distinct evidence of his virility in bathing trunks, her imagination retreated from his full nakedness. Or tried to retreat. The compulsion to look was overpowering. She compromised, seeing him desexed, as shorn of maleness as if he'd undergone surgery. There was a kind of horror about the image that made her skin crawl and filled her with anxiety.

Between Sacramento and Vallejo it became light enough to turn off her headlights. She turned them on again in Oakland because fog covered the bay area like a grounded cloud. While she was crossing the miles-long Bay Bridge to San Francisco on the upper level and listening to the trucks and electric trains on the deck below and the weird orchestration of foghorns, signal buoys and klaxons rising from the invisible bay, the horror image of Larry reappeared.

By the time she parked the Jag in its port behind the tower apartment building in the Lake Merced area it was past 6:30. She lugged her things in to the elevator in two trips, then rode up to the seventh floor and set them off. She got them into her one-bedroom apartment in two trips.

During a lifetime of arrivals and departures from boarding schools, camps, country and city houses and apartments, Florida and Maine cottages, Mexican and Hawaiian and European resort hotels and villas, she'd formed the habit of unpacking immediately.

Going to a new place, or, equally, returning to an old one, she always had an uneasy feel of temporariness, of being a stranger, of not belonging there, until some of the drawer and closet space was personalized by her things. Automatically now, she began to unpack. *How damned silly!* she thought, and stopped herself. Within half an hour she would be preparing to go and live with Larry. . . .

She paced restlessly into the large, smartly furnished living-dining area. She opened the picture window drapes and couldn't see the ground for the fog. She went into the compact kitchen, wanting some soup and toast. She couldn't settle long enough to prepare it. Her hunger was for something indefinable. Her unpacked things nag-nag-nagged at her until she finally gave in.

Within ten minutes she had everything transferred to its proper place, soiled things in laundry and cleaner bags. The action calmed her somehow, giving her a sense of—she made a vague, trailing gesture—she didn't know exactly what. As a child she'd needed that sense of—orderliness? stability? permanence? safety? virtue? To try now to achieve it by going through a routine was empty ritual and neurotic. Like applying bandages to wounds healed long ago.

She stood motionless in the center of the solid-color, pinkish-gray carpet in the sitting room with her back to New York, staring out the picture window into the fog. It was almost seven here now and almost ten in New York. In mere minutes Larry would be reaching his desk. Waiting time was standstill time, heavy time.

An emotion she hadn't experienced in years and which she'd considered dead returned, as potent and unbearable as ever. There was a frightful coldness and heaviness in her chest, filling her like solid lead. But as that vile, long-ago governess had proven, lead was meltable. It yielded to warmth that began slow and sweet and insidiously increased and became feverish excitement.

Now, staring unblinkingly out at the fog she was unaware that her hands had moved. They were resting there on the center front of her skirt. She frowned down at herself—*clean, mannerly, pretty little girls did not do that*—and dropped her hands to her sides. A moment later she scowled defiantly, kicked off her shoes and went over and got the telephone. She carried it to the sofa, settled herself in one corner with her legs tucked up under her, and placed the person-to-person call to Larry.

After a minute the connection was made with his office switchboard.

34

"Irina?" His voice came thrillingly across the continent and she squirmed, blinked, sat straighter, a little shiver running down the back of her neck.

"Larry!" she said in an anxious rush. "Oh, it's so good to hear you. How are you, Larry?"

"Why, fine. Fine, dear. What's wrong?" he said worriedly. "Is something wrong, Irina?"

"Oh, no. No, Larry!"

"Are you sure?"

"Of course, Larry. Don't worry. That's the last thing I'd want to cause you, you know that. What I called about . . . what I called about was. . ."

"Take your time, Irina," he said in that deep, patient, soothing, all-embracing, understanding voice. "Take a breath."

She drew in a breath, her mouth close to the mouthpiece so he might hear her obedience.

"Well, you see, Larry, you see. . ." Again her words began to tumble over each other. He laughed quietly, a broadly rolling, warm sound and she could almost feel the caress of his hand on her forehead and temple. She knew just what he'd say and he did.

"Now, now, you mustn't get overexcited. There's no hurry. I've got all the time in the world to hear anything you have to say."

She started to scrape her lower lip with her teeth and she could feel her face coloring and her eyes started to burn.

"I know. I know," she said, blinking back tears. "You always did have time. You were the only one in the world who cared enough."

"No," he said gently.

"Well, if you say so."

"You and I licked those old problems. We shouldn't have to go back into them. We know why you weren't always the kind of little girl you wanted to be. You misbehaved to attract attention."

"Still and all, Larry, I didn't have to be that way for *you* to see me. You saw the best in me at once and made it easy to come up to it. That was so valuable to me, I became something I couldn't have, otherwise. . . ." She broke off, sweating, her scalp prickling. Since then—he had no idea—she'd gone backward, because alone, sep-

35

arated from him, she was no good. "Larry, I didn't mean to rehash the past. What I called about was . . . was . . ."

How could she make such a shocking proposition! He had never made the slightest gesture of sexual interest, neither looking at nor touching her intimately. Never! He was proud to be her counsel and friend and guide and protector and he saw "his favorite" as lovely and fine. Her skin crawled at the thought of losing that stature in his eyes, of selling it out for the sake of some taboo, ugly thrill. Oh, no! She sat shaking, her teeth chattering.

"Larry, listen. There wasn't any reason and I'm ashamed for calling you, taking up your valuable time, being dependent and . . . All I wanted was to hear you and know you're there and all right and let you know how much I miss you. Oh, I sometimes miss you *so* much."

"I know you do. And I miss you. Please don't cry."

"All right."

"You're too emotional, Irina."

"Yes."

"You're there by your own decision, remember. And I know you're fully capable of disciplining yourself. And I'm counting on your studying hard, maturing, increasing your natural abilities in every way. And although I was very proud of the motives that got you expelled before graduation from that secondary school, I won't be if you fail to earn your college degree."

"I'll make you proud."

"Promise me."

"I promise. And when I promise you anything, I never break it. I never fail. I'm never bad. I'm just the girl you require me to be and I'm good because you're good. Larry, say what I am."

"You're my favorite."

"Once more."

"You're my favorite."

She gave a long sigh.

"I'll ring off now. I feel all straightened out again. I've been fine and I'll take care of myself . . . uh, but, Larry. . ." she said hesitantly.

"What?"

"Would you not mention it that I called?"

"Well . . . all right. I understand. I won't. Good-bye, Irina."

" 'Bye."

She hung up and dropped her head back against the sofa back, closing her eyes and letting bliss stroke over her in healing waves, thinking with a soft fervor that she would gladly die for him. Or submit to any torture, any deprivation.

After a while she trudged into the bedroom and undressed. She looked at her naked body and saw a *woman's* beauty. But she hadn't dared assert the fact. The phone call had been a farce reducing her to childhood. She crawled under the bedcovers and hid her face in the pillow, loathing herself. Because, underlying her retreat to virtue was fear, even dread, of her mother.

chapter four

Until she was four, Irina remembered, she'd never questioned her brother Noel's authority over her. Mostly he played with other boys, but often enough with her and Elly, and he was almost always fun. The only times she wouldn't be proud of him was when he was around his mother and he'd get bossy or whiny if he didn't have his way exactly or wasn't winning. She was loyal to him against their cousins and the children of their parents' friends and would never have thought of tattling on him even when he got mad and hit her.

One time when a beautiful girl cousin Noel's age was visiting and enchanting all the adults with her dancing and singing and Noel had caught her secretly and kicked her pants, Irina had lied so hard to save him from a spanking that she'd got one along with him.

When he began kindergarten she missed him and couldn't wait for him to get home for lunch. Then he would tell importantly everything that had happened. More, he taught her the songs and games he learned. Regular games and secret ones.

There was one he made her play when she was supposed to be having a nap. He would come in and be the doctor and she would be naked and he would keep frowning like he didn't like her. Pretty soon she wouldn't be just playing sick but really feeling sick. If she said she didn't want to play, he would pinch her and hurt her so bad she'd cry. It was never any fun. Finally she said she had to be the doctor and that game stopped.

Another game was husband and wife, when he'd lay on top of her, both with their clothes on. There were variations on that, including divorces when he'd let her be the wife of one or another of his friends. Being hugged and kissed and laid on top of and bouncing and giggling on the bed had been fun. But most of all she had liked the scary ritual of being sworn to secrecy and knowing she was part of a conspiracy. But she didn't know there was anything secret about boys. She'd never had more than a side or back glimpse of one naked until that September a week after she was four.

The war was on, her father was an army major stationed in Washington, and they'd moved to a house in commuting distance of the District. Noel began imagining himself a part of the adult world and too far advanced to even notice her. His mother had brought him a miniature army officer's uniform with oak leaves on the shoulders like his father's and he enjoyed putting it on and strutting around.

He carried a swagger stick and got in the habit of whacking the backs of her and Elly's legs if they didn't hop lively when he told them to do something. He had a roomful of war toys and he'd let her step in and look, then chase her out. Or if he and his friends needed Nazis to bomb and sink and shoot at, they'd be brought in. Elly would cry, but Irina would get mad and start kicking and throwing the Allied Forces all over the room, sending Noel into a rage.

One Saturday their mother had had lunch with them all. Irina had proposed that she and Elly go upstairs and watch her dress for going out. Their mother had said she was in a hurry; but a minute later Noel went up and walked in and was allowed to stay. When he came out he'd got a playful squirt from his mother's perfume atomizer.

Irina had laughed and whispered to Elly, "He smells like a girl."

Elly laughed so hard she had to hold her stomach.

Noel scowled and tapped Elly on the head with his swagger stick.

38

"Whattaya think you're laughing at?"

At that moment her mother came hurrying down the stairs, calling: "Come kiss Mother good-bye, Irina and Elly pet."

Elly ran to her. Irina stood where she was.

"Irina, I haven't got all day."

"Well, you can just wave to me."

"Well, you can just *walk* to me."

She walked over.

"I won't kiss a scowling face!"

Irina smiled. Her mother kissed her cheek. Irina wiped her cheek, turned and walked three steps. She anticipated the whack on the seat of her pants and had a blood-curdling scream going before it landed. She dropped to a sitting position on the floor and howled.

"Ow-woooh . . . oouch, oh, you hurt me!"

"I did not."

Irina beat the floor with her fists. "You did, you *did*. . . . you hate me. You didn't squirt me with perfume. You let him gobble up *my* birthday cake, and didn't give me a uniform, too. He made me and Elly be Nazis. He hit Elly on the head with that mean stick!"

"I didn't."

"You did."

"He did, too," Elly chimed in. She sat down and cried and held the top of her head.

"Noel, you're not to hit your little sister! Here, come to Mother, baby." She picked Elly up and kissed the top of her head. "Now it's well. Irina, get up from there and quit making a silly scene. I didn't hurt you, and you know it, don't you?"

"Yes." Irina sighed and got up.

When her mother had gone Noel sneered at Irina.

"Ha ha, if you thought she'd give in and buy *you* a uniform."

"You smell like a girl, Noel Devereaux. You're nothing but a girl with perfume on. You wear that officer cap around here all the time because your hair's long like a girl's."

"Stupid!" He pulled off the cap to prove how short his hair was.

"Anyway you're a girl."

"I'll slap you if you say that, Irina."

"I'll still think it."

He suddenly hopped up and down in a rage. He grabbed her arm and pulled her up the stairs and into his room.

"You sit right down there. I'll show you."

And he had. He took his trousers and shorts off and faced her. For a while she couldn't say a thing or do anything but stare. She couldn't believe her eyes.

Finally she demanded angrily, "Where'd you get that?"

"Boy, you're dumb. Didn't even know what boys look like."

"I'm like that, too."

He guffawed. "You liar."

"Well, I will be when I'm six."

"You will not. You have to be born that way. And you weren't. You're nothing but a girl. Nothing!"

"I don't believe you."

"Ask anybody. Everybody knows. Except you and Elly."

"You think I won't ask. I will. And, boy, you'll wish you didn't lie, Noel Devereaux. You'll be sorry. You're like that because there's something wrong with you. You got a disease."

She didn't remember how she became convinced he wasn't lying, but she had. She'd resented having such a secret kept from her and was outraged by the injustice of boys having something special that she couldn't have. She brooded and found it unpleasant to be near him.

In the past when they got mad they couldn't think of one good thing about the other, but soon enough they'd be in another mood and couldn't think of one bad thing. The one continuing thing was a feeling that they belonged to each other. So even if she didn't like it, she never questioned his right to hurt her because he'd be on her side if anybody else—except his mother—did.

And she would be on his side and be sorry and loving when he needed her to be, because she felt that way. She didn't *intend* to stop being sorry and loving. It was just that she didn't feel that way any more after finding out about his maleness.

He got mad about it. And madder. Then maddest the time he fell and skinned his knee bloody. The governess clucked and bandaged him. Elly looked sad and patted him and rubbed her own knee and said, "Poor Noel . . . Poor Noel. . . My knee hurts, too."

Irina had been standing by, expressionless. When Elly said that she started to laugh. "Your knee doesn't either hurt."

"It does, too!" Noel shouted. "Don't listen to Irina."

"You better listen to me!" Irina warned her. Elly looked down at her knee, then at Noel, then at Irina, not knowing if her knee hurt or not. The governess stepped in and took Elly away. Noel glared at Irina.

"You don't care if I'm hurt."

"Why don't you tell on me?"

"I will! You just wait till Mother gets home."

Preparations for a grown-up party that night had everybody bustling. There was a general easy-laughing mood and Irina was allowed to watch the tables being set in the main dining room, and to stay in the kitchen and get tastes of everything. When stern Miss Burkhardt, the governess, came looking for her to take her nap, the maids and cook hid her in a pantry for a while, though of course she was found and marched up to bed and lectured about the way little ladies should behave. When it was dark she and Elly were bathed and dressed for supper in plain dresses. Later they would be all dressed up and be shown off to the grownups.

Her new pink dress with the satin bow and her hair ribbons and her new pink socks with tiny silver edging were all so beautiful and exciting she couldn't wait. Meantime she was so hungry her mouth was watering. Then about two minutes before she and Elly and Noel would go down to their supper her mother sent for her.

Her mother was about to get dressed and had on a negligee you could see through and nothing else but panties and a brassiere. A maid was moving around the room and a long shiny pale-blue gown lay across the bed. Her mother was painting her lips, and her hair had been done for the party and was piled up on top of her head, black and shiny and very tall, and there were jewels laid out on the long mirrored dressing table.

She looked even more special and beautiful than the glass and silver and napkins and tablecloths and vases of flowers in the main dining room and Irina looked at her, marveling. Her mother had put down her lipstick brush and reached for a diamond earring and screwed it on at the same time, without looking directly at her, she had talked in a quiet, disapproving voice

41

that was worse than a scolding. Noel had told on her, because she hadn't felt sorry about him hurting his knee.

The way her mother talked it would have been better if she'd been to blame for his hurting himself. Not to feel the way a nice sister should feel was a sort of hopeless badness. Irina went to supper feeling ugly and mean. She couldn't eat a bite or look at Noel and Elly. Miss Burkhardt said if she didn't eat she'd have to leave the table even before her father came to have dessert with them. She went to her room and sat on the bed. When it was time to dress up and go downstairs she refused.

But Miss Burkhardt undressed and redressed her. When she had on all her pretty clothes her face stayed miserable. The skirt of the pink dress was gauzy and so short it showed her panties. Standing on a chair while Miss Burkhardt turned the cuffs of the new socks, Irina looked down at her legs and felt bare and ugly.

"I don't want anybody to see me. I'm ugly."

"If you're trying to make me say you're pretty," Miss Burkhardt said, stroking her legs, then rubbing and patting the seat of her panties, "I will. You're pretty. Pretty as a doll, and sweet as sugar. Now will you smile for me?"

"No."

"Please?" She kissed her upper leg lightly, then comically licked her lips. "Sweet as sugar . . . And still my little mistress won't smile?"

"I *can't!*"

Miss Burkhardt turned and went out of the room. She came back in and locked the door. She was carrying a section of newspaper and began to roll it. She used a rolled newspaper often as a kind of stick of authority, and whether she merely brandished it or swatted painlessly Irina hated it. Watching Miss Burkhardt come she scowled.

But, astonishingly, Miss Burkhardt took Irina's hand and folded it around the rolled newspaper and said in a low, hasty voice, "So that you'll feel good and smile when you go downstairs we'll play a secret game. You've got the whip and you're boss and I have to do just exactly what you tell me to. All right? Now . . . What do I have to do? Are you going to make me kiss your feet?"

Before Irina could catch up with what was happening Miss Burkhardt bent and kissed the tips of her black patent shoes. Then she looked up, her eyes bright.

"Is that enough? Or must I kiss you here, too?" she whispered while her hand was stroking Irina's panties, then patting and pinching softly. "Do I have to . . . are you going to beat me if I don't?"

"Yes!" Irina wagged the rolled paper.

"I won't do it . . . you can't make me. Not unless you hit me."

Irina hit her in the face with the paper.

"Please don't beat me! I'll do it, I'll do it!"

"You better!"

Irina turned and pushed her bottom out to be kissed and when Miss Burkhardt actually did it she began to giggle and hop up and down on the chair.

Miss Burkhardt watched her and sighed and shook her head. "Ah, how cute you are . . . how delicious . . ." She took the rolled newspaper from her, then caught her up and hugged her.

"Now I have to give you up and let others look at you. But they're not allowed to see my little flower in the bath and they can never know how really beautiful you are the way I do, eh?"

"I thought you don't even like me."

"Oh, of course you thought that. But I love you. I love you so much I want to kiss you all the time. But it has to be a secret. They would send me away if they found out I love you more than Noel and the little one. So when they are watching us we have to pretend. And so I will scold and discipline you and not smile at you the way I want to. . . . But in secret! Well, you'll see, Irina. You'll see. Now, let's go and get the other children and go downstairs. You mustn't tell anybody about the game we just played—or the ones we will play in the future."

"All right."

When she and Noel and Elly went in, the grownups were having cocktails and snacks and everybody fussed over them. Both she and Elly were picked up and kissed lots of times. But after a while her father had Elly in his arms and Noel was sitting in his mother's chair with her and Irina decided to see if they would even notice if she wasn't there. She moved a little way toward the edge of the room, then a little more, then she went out through the wide doorway into the hall.

She backed off farther and farther and just stood waiting and waiting and watching and watching and nobody noticed for a long time. When somebody did notice, it was too late because her chest was full of lead, and she felt ugly and sick at her stomach and she knew she was so bad that she should die.

In bed she couldn't sleep for a long time, and when she did she woke up crying. Miss Burkhardt kept looking in on her and finally brought a tray of food and sat coaxing her to eat, bite by bite. Still she couldn't sleep and then Miss Burkhardt came back in and got into bed with her and took her pajamas off her and began to stroke her and kiss her from the tips of her toes to her shoulders. It felt very soothing.

Then she began to do something else and that felt good and made her warm all over. She kept doing it and the warm feeling became hot and fast and she began to lurch and heave on the bed and she got scared and dizzy and she was so excited she wanted to yell and then she got scared and tried to push her away.

Miss Burkhardt held her tighter and she made funny noises and breathed very fast. . . . Irina kept pushing at her and finally she quit. The next thing Irina knew she was waking up and it was daylight and what had happened was so strange she couldn't believe it.

Through that day and the next and the next, Miss Burkhardt was just the same stern, prissy thing she always had been, even during her baths. Then again she came in the night and did it to her.

For a while afterward the governess did it every night and at nap time, too. There were other periods when days, even weeks, went by without its happening. But the concealed relationship never stopped completely till after Irina was five and Miss Burkhardt was discharged or quit, she never knew which.

During the early part of the perverted affair she struck back at Noel. For some reason or other he'd got her down and hit her and made her cry. Afterward she wouldn't make up. She remembered how Noel had got a bad spanking over their cousin when he'd kicked her and pulled her hair (and how she had got herself spanked, too, for his sake).

She decided to get him spanked. When her father came to her room to say good night at bedtime she begged him to stay. She petted his uniform and kept looking up in

44

his face and said what Elly said: "You're so pretty, Daddy," to make him grin. She came up out of the covers and stood hugging him and kissing him and being sweet to him till he was laughing and petting and kissing her, and saying she was a little vamp and a flirt and a doll-girl.

Then she pouted and lowered her lashes and started to tell him how Noel was always hitting and hurting her and making her cry. She would look up every once in a while and see that her father's round, pink face was getting more and more mad at Noel. He said he would speak to that young man, but Irina knew Noel wouldn't care about that, so she said Noel hurt her worse than he really did, and her daddy got real nice and mean-looking and went out of the room.

About a minute later she could hear her father and mother yelling at each other in Noel's room. Then her father was roaring and her mother shut up. Irina sat listening, grinning and wide-eyed. Pretty soon Noel was getting it good and screaming his head off and crying, and begging his father to quit and promising to be good.

Next afternoon Noel had to stay in his room. When his mother left the house Irina went in.

"Ha, ha, cry-baby got a spanking and has to stay in his room."

"You get out!" He yelled and ran to her. She jumped away.

"I dare you to hit me. I dare you." She ran and he ran after her. "I made him spank you. And if you don't be good I'll make him again."

He stopped and glowered at her. She stood looking at him, then she stepped a little closer.

"Dare you," she said. He didn't do anything. She stepped closer yet, close enough for him to hit her. He didn't. "Ha, ha, ha! Scaredy-cat . . . Sissy . . . Girl . . . Cry-baby . . . Tattletale little mama's boy . . ."

He shut his eyes and jumped at her with both hands out, hitting her chest and knocking her down. She began to cry and Miss Burkhardt came in and took her out and shook her finger at Noel.

That evening Noel got another spanking. The next day she went and rubbed it in again. He sulked and tried to ignore her and didn't dare hit her. In the future, whenever he lost his temper he regretted it. He gradually learned that he just thought he was bigger than she was

45

and that in reality she had the power to make him cry louder than he could make her cry.

It got so he didn't want to strike out at her even with words, and if she was assertive enough about anything with him he would finally back away. Especially while Miss Burkhardt was still there, she had a gleeful sense of secretly carrying a magic wand . . . like a rolled newspaper.

In a queer way her changing relationship with Noel was an imitation of the one with Miss Burkhardt. Both were bigger, stronger, but secretly ruled by her. On the surface and in the daylight and so far as the world knew, the governess governed, but at night she yielded up all her size and strength and authority.

Irina hadn't grasped the truth of her own superior position at once because at first the woman, like an emotional vulture, had seen and moved in on moods of distress when Irina had felt somehow abandoned and ugly, unloved and unlovable. No matter that it had been perversion; it had had the feel to her child senses of something that banished pain and brought pleasure, and therefore it was good. And Miss Burkhardt always kept telling her privately how beautiful she was, how she loved her more than anything in the world and that what she was giving her was the right and good and needed thing.

But during the day when Miss Burkhardt was being boss she was unsmiling and unloving and strict. She watched her table manners and would lecture her about the proper way to act and speak and if she caught her, or Elly, touching themselves privately she was very mean about it. Irina furiously resented that particular discipline of not being allowed to handle herself, as if it was bad and dirty, when all the time Miss Burkhardt did worse to her.

After one of those reproofs Irina hated her and when she came at night she wouldn't let herself be touched. She found out that the governess wanted to do what she did to her more than Irina wanted her to, because she pleaded. She groveled and begged. She let herself be hit without hitting back. And progressively through the months she submitted to all kinds of punishments, like being kicked and walked on and sat on and made to stand in a corner, or whatever Irina could think up.

And if she didn't think things up, Miss Burkhardt did.

Really terrible things that made her cry tears—like sticking a pin in her and pinching and burning her with a match. Miss Burkhardt would sometimes get like a wild animal and she'd be scared and suddenly know she was powerless and couldn't stop the woman.

She couldn't yet figure out why she'd never told her father or mother, because she really came to fear the governess. On the other hand, there was something druglike and dreadfully fascinating about it all, even when it wasn't fun. She got even more nervous than she had been before, and it was a relief when the woman was gone from her life. But Noel was still there and she liked the feel of his being scared of her, and occasions would come up every few months when she didn't just threaten, but demonstrated her power to have him whipped and make him cry.

Then there was a period of a few years when she and Noel and Elly were only together during vacations because they were in different boarding schools. They never had any special troubles, but she was always getting suspended or expelled.

The funny part of it was she really liked learning and got along fine with the other girls and had a lot of friends in each school. Furthermore, teachers and headmistresses liked her and she liked them.

However, there were set routines and rules and musts of one kind and another and just being aware of anything she *must* not do was a challenge. So she would do it and earn demerits and punishments. Then, just to show everybody she wasn't going to be scared or tamed, she'd break more rules.

The teachers who were so nice were really enforcers and she disliked their using their niceness to bring her into line and she became a specialist at impudence, insolence and disrespect. One headmistress had booted her out and summed her up in a way Irina appreciated: "Persistent and unrepentant disobedience."

She had to spend a lot of summertime with tutors. The summer she was nine and Elly eight, her little sister started assuming a high-nosed, prissy attitude of superior virtue. She was always mincing around in "adorable" little dresses with her long blond hair beribboned daintily and she cooed in the presence of adults and acted like she thought she was an ornament on a cake.

They were in Maine at the time, in a big cottage near Kennebunkport, and one morning the cake icing consented to go walking down the beach with Irina. They wore little swim suits and while Irina was red and skinny, Elly was tanned and plump.

"You sure have a pretty tan, Elly."

"Oh, yes, my complexion is very nice. You sure get funny-looking when you're sunburned. Maybe I could let you use my oil."

"Maybe you could. Is it a sweet oil? Is that what makes everybody think you're sweet as sugar?"

"What're you looking like that at me for? I'm going back."

"No you're not. We're going to go swimming."

"Not in the ocean we're not. It's not safe and it's cold."

They stopped near the edge of the water and Irina started to grin at her.

"Scared you'll melt?"

Elly started to turn and Irina grabbed her arm and yanked and backed into the icy water. Elly tried to pull loose and fell on her behind and screamed; "You let me alone."

Irina held on and pulled her by the arm, and by the hair, too. She, herself, was knee-deep in the water and Elly was in a half-sitting, floundering sprawl, squealing that it was cold and fighting to get free. Irina let her get up, then tackled her around the knees and flopped them both into the water, wrestling.

Irina held her down in the muddy sand and sloshed water in her face and then growled, "I'm going to drown you."

Irina caught her by the foot and dragged her out deeper till she was floating. Then she dropped under the surface and grabbed Elly and pulled her down. She let her up almost at once. Elly got to her feet, waist-deep, her hair plastered around her face. Her eyes were terrified and she just held her mouth open, stunned. Irina jeered.

"Boy, if you could see yourself you wouldn't think you were so pretty."

Then, before Elly could get ashore Irina dropped again and pulled her legs out from under her and she sat down, under water. Irina helped her up, then pushed her down, then lifted her, then pushed her down. She was spluttering

48

and blue-lipped before she dragged her out on the sand. Elly lay there and Irina sat beside her.

Elly rolled away, crying. Irina jerked her and put her on her back. She climbed on her, straddling her with her knees and sat on her stomach.

"Know what I'm going to do when you're asleep?" she demanded. Elly just stared. "You better answer if you don't want me to fill your mouth and nose with sand."

"What?" Elly said, her face miserable, her mouth quivering.

"That's better. I'm going to come in the night when you're asleep and put a live lobster in your bed and—" she reached back of her to Elly's crotch and pinched— "it'll pinch. Like that, only worse. You scared of lobster claws?" She poised her hands, curved like claws, above Elly's face. "Huh?"

"Yes. Please don't, Irina. What do you want to be mean to me for?" She pouted her mouth.

"Because I hate you."

"You don't either!" Elly started to whimper like a baby.

"I do. You think because I used to like you that I don't hate you. I do. I'll kill you sometime. That's what I'll do. When you tell on me now and I get a whipping, I'll run away. I'll go and hide in New York City where nobody'll find me. And I'll wait and when you come back to the city I'll get you. Or maybe I'll do it in Philadelphia. Or I'll come to your boarding school. With a gun. And a knife. Or, maybe I'll put poison in your food. I'll do it if you tell."

"I won't tell."

Irina let her up and she ran like mad, screaming at the top of her voice. Irina didn't follow. She stayed out all day. When they came looking for her she expected to get a real whipping. But Elly hadn't told.

Suddenly she loved her and was sorry for her and she hated herself. And she got Elly aside and kissed and hugged her and then—well, she didn't know why, maybe because of the quiet, heartbroken way Elly cried and clung lovingly to her—well, then she'd suddenly hit her in the stomach with her fist as hard as she could. The minute she did that mean thing she got meaner, bending down and threatening her with all kinds of horrors if she wasn't good.

She did sneaking, terrifying things to Elly all sum-

49

mer long. She would be sorry every time, for a little while
. . . and then she would do it again. The poor little fool
couldn't ever believe Irina would do such things to her.
She kept on *loving* her, and believed as hard as she could
that Irina still loved her.

One time she almost tripped her at the top of the stairs
and might have broken her neck, and just at the last
instant she'd stopped herself. Noel had been in the hall
and she thought he saw what had been in her mind and
she went and picked a fight with him. And although he
was a head taller and had had boxing lessons and knew
she couldn't get him spanked any more, he backed up
and let her hit him all she wanted to.

All he did was protect his face and wait, knowing that
she just had a little mad on and would work it out soon.
But if he hit her and turned the little mad into a big one,
he wasn't sure he could handle her. The disgrace of losing
to a girl was more than he would risk. He had good
reason to be wary. He was only capable of anger, she
of fury.

The things she did to Elly made her ashamed because
she was coldly calculating about them and knew just what
she was doing. The awful part of it was that she wasn't
really like that. She'd found out in schools and on visits
and at parties that there were girls who were naturally
mean and deliberately picked on smaller girls and hurt
dogs and kittens and she would never be friends with
hateful things like that.

After she herself had been a hateful thing she wanted
to suffer, but feeling sorry wasn't suffering—in fact, there
was something about that aching feeling that was warm
and sweet and pleasant. So she made herself really hurt.
For instance, she poured two cups half full of salt, then
bit and tore her fingernails to the raw bleeding quick and
plunged her fingers into the salt. And she would hold
them there while the pain, like acid eating into her flesh,
went scalding relentlessly through her whole body making her cry.

One night in her bathroom she took a pack of twenty
matches and was going to light every one of them and
burn herself. By the time she had five blisters on her
behind she was dancing in silent agony and almost biting
clear through her forearm to keep from screaming.

50

She'd had a sense of being her own law. When at the end of that summer, after her tenth birthday, she was in a new school away from Elly, she had an impulse to hurt herself. After she did it she got to giggling because she realized this time she hadn't done anything to Elly to make her punish herself. Therefore she was ahead of the game and it would be necessary the next time she saw Elly to even things up.

She'd never been sexually unaware since Miss Burkhardt. The woman's overstimulation of the private region of her body had undoubtedly increased the local blood supply and system of nerves. She was not only extra-sensitive there but more developed physically than most girls her age. Against the general skimpiness of her build the fullness of that intimate area was noticeable.

When she wore an unskirted bathing suit or too snug shorts she was acutely conscious of the boys' fascinated, often very direct, stares. Even when the focus of this interest was totally concealed in a modest dress there was a certain precocity reflected in her face, no matter what kind of expression she wore. She did not have to simper or smile or flirt; she was far more likely to frown and reject their attentions.

Nonetheless, wherever there were boys she was noticed; at the little dancing parties they gave her no rest and during kissing games they'd get positively silly and no matter how nastily she conducted herself they wouldn't let her alone. They didn't merely like to kiss and hug her, but tried to feel her or get peeks under her skirt.

By eleven she was a sophisticated junior siren. Once at a kid party she carried her rug, towel and basket to the empty end of a private beach. She sat her seventy pounds down and tipped the whole party toward her because the boys, playing games and showing off, began to slide down her way and the girls had to follow.

The family vacationed in Honolulu the Christmas she was thirteen. She was supple as rubber and learned the hula easily as if her hips had always known it instinctively. At a big luau she painted her whole body Hawaiian brown and put on a grass skirt and leis and pinned white flowers in her black hair. She got into the mood of the singing and chanting and the stroking waves of firelight and the rhythm movement of her own hips, and

51

she was aware of people watching her and of the music getting faster and faster and carrying her until she seemed to be shaking herself to pieces.

A whole line of girls and women were dancing and there was a competition flavor to see who could last the longest and she won . . . and then kept on and on in a state of delicious frenzy till they stopped her. She was so feverish and shaky she couldn't calm down later.

At spring vacation they were at an island resort in the Caribbean, her parents and her mother's personal maid in one cottage, she and Elly and an elderly maid in another. She took to sneaking cosmetics out to the beach. Once she sat alone in a swimming suit. She had on eyeshadow and lipstick and she painted her fingernails and toenails and wore bracelets and an anklet. She sat stroking oil onto her legs very slowly and paying no obvious attention to two older teen-age couples. But she kept looking at one of the boys, who was about seventeen, and he kept looking at her.

The elderly maid had caught her all decorated up that way and marched her to her mother and a group of friends sunning themselves and drinking on a terrace. All the women had got the giggles looking at her. She'd been deplumed. But the teen boy from the beach didn't lose interest. He followed her around all over the hotel grounds. She snooted him and led him on at the same time.

He caught her on a little ornamental footbridge one evening and kissed her and stuck his tongue in her mouth. While he was doing it he pressed her against the railing of the bridge so that she would feel his lower body against hers and she started doing something like the hula, there while he was kissing her, moving her hips and feeling very warm and devilish and something shocking happened to his body, as if he grew in one minute from boy to man and he was hurting her.

An older girl in school had described how such a thing happened to a man and changed him and made him wonderfully exciting. . . . But it seemed terrible and dangerous and she pushed him and walked away fast. He followed her and was very shaky and persistent and begged to kiss her again, but she wouldn't let him till he promised not to do what he had done.

He gave his solemn word but the minute he was pressing against her he did it again. He pleaded that he couldn't help it, and he couldn't. She tested him several times in the next few days. He asked her to do something and she slapped his mouth for saying that word. But she liked hearing him say it and tempted him into saying it several times, slapping him each time. She regretted when his vacation was done and he went away.

After that experience, her contempt for boys her own age was boundless. She went after boys who weren't mere boys any more. She even tried being very loving to Noel for a while to try and find out if he was a man. But he wouldn't kiss her.

In May, a few weeks before she would have completed the semester she got expelled from her boarding school. Her mother was on a trip somewhere and the house wasn't open, so she was sent to the Philadelphia home of her mother's parents. She took a night train and slept fitfully, dreaming about an endless journey through an unknown frightening nowhere. Her train got in very early and Uncle Jack, one of her mother's two older brothers, met her, looking as if he'd just come from a party.

He was his usual gusty, unserious self and seeing her he stretched out his arms and said laughingly, "Hi, bad girl, come to your bad uncle."

He folded her in to him when she ran to his arms and gave her a hug and pats on the shoulders and a kiss. "My little wildflower beauty did it again, and bedamned to 'em, eh?"

She shook her head, gazing up at him miserably, then suddenly she wrapped herself around him and cried, her whole body going limp.

"Now, now, don't go spaghetti on me. Where's that wiry defiance? We can't whip the Redcoats that way! While all the nice schoolgirls are droning away, you and I will buzz!"

"I just want to go back to school," she whimpered, clinging. "I counted so much on finishing the year!"

She'd slept most of the day. At dinner, her grandparents didn't get scoldy, which depressed her. It was as if they'd given up on her. She didn't see them much more than once a day after that; and because she refused all Uncle Jack's offers to amuse her she saw little of him.

Her mother came and at another time her father came,

53

each staying overnight, then going away and leaving her there. She sensed, and later knew, that there was trouble between her parents which would come to divorce in a few months. The whole future was up in the air. But she liked the Philadelphia place and was more than content to stay there.

chapter five

The house was large, very old and famous. Historical societies and civic groups sent tours through it regularly. Within was the reconstructed original house and furnishings that dated back to Revolutionary War times. There were all sorts of preserved documents and newspapers and pictures and uniforms and banners and insignias and swords, muskets, even a cannon, from the past. There was a portrait gallery of famous ancestors who'd been generals, admirals, governors, senators, ambassadors and, most famous of all, a signer of the Declaration of Independence.

As a little girl Irina had looked forward to dressing up and inserting herself into the tours and being introduced as a direct lineal descendant of the signer of the Declaration. Other areas of the house were impressive, too, with rooms full of priceless tapestries and rugs too fine to step on and there were displays of marvelous old furniture and others of vases and silversmithing. The place was like a big museum with an attached boarding house. There were apartments on upper floors for her grandparents and for Uncle Jack and for visiting families or relatives.

Of all the grandchildren, Irina was the only one who enjoyed staying there. This fact, considering she was the brattiest and should have hated its gloominess, was looked on as a quirk by everybody but Uncle Jack. He'd been a brat, too, and he, too, had a curious attachment to the house.

He began going with her to the various family-history rooms and discussing the past in a solemn way which was unlike everything else she knew about him. He'd always drunk too much, chased women, jumped all over the world being what her mother called "the disgusting kind of rich irresponsible playboy." He'd got into and out of four marriages and forty affairs.

At times he "settled down," used his hereditary position on the boards of the family businesses to push for disruptive innovations, then run out on what he'd started, leaving a mess to be cleaned up while he amused himself with a new adventure.

Since Irina could remember, he'd been popping into their lives unexpectedly, bringing surprise presents and giving the children parties and throwing their lives into delicious commotion. He'd gone to special pains to provide her thrills: taking her in his private airplane, on his shoulders on water skis, in his arms off fifteen- and twenty-foot diving boards, for sails across bays and lakes at a clip and a tilt that "wet their backsides," and he'd got her into a racing boat and racing cars, too. He gave off energy and excitement like a dynamo.

She'd always loved the physical feel of him and never let him know she was scared of anything even if she was quaking. She was proud when he got decorated in the war and wasn't surprised, the way everybody else was, that he made such a good fighting man. He was laughing and handsome with curly brown hair and his mouth was so kissable that she understood completely why all the girls were crazy about him.

His solemn manner with her when she was thirteen made him even more attractive. More and more often he had her up to his apartment on the fourth floor for afternoon "tea." Some afternoons he was barely out of bed, complaining of a hangover. Usually he was glad to see her and often talked about the house.

"It's strange," he mused one afternoon, "but I never had any other home; even when I was married and had other houses. I always have the sense that this is *me,* that when I'm here where I belong I'm in the direct line of all my—*our*—worthwhile ancestors. It gives me a sense of continuity, of meaning. And you have the same understanding of what you really are when you're here, Irina."

"I think I do, too, Uncle Jack. I never feel mean and ugly here. I feel all of the importance of this house is part of me, too, and that I'm a good person, not a . . . well, not what I *really* am."

"What you *really* are is what you feel here, too. You

55

know what it is that I think you and I understand about our ancestry that none of the others do?"

"Yes."

"Yes? . . . Well, all right, let's hear."

"They signed the Declaration of Independence. They defied the proper authorities. They fought them. That was greatness. But it was considered wicked by the authorities."

"You hit it, Irina. You *know*. *I* know. But who else knows? Our contemporaries, including those who trace back to that splendid defiance and assertion, have taken on the characteristics of the oppressors. Rebel against their conventions and they brand you criminal or sinner. If we could time-transplant these people as they are now back into the boots of their ancestors, they'd be *horrified* by the insane proposition of defying the mother country."

"They'd fight on the side of the Redcoats against anybody like us . . . and we're the ones that *created* this country."

He looked at her proudly.

"Why couldn't I have met a woman like you?"

She shrugged, smiling with pleasure.

"You know what we are, Irina? The only ones who carry the hot blood that made us free. We're alive in the wrong century. We retain the fervor and the courage meant for other times. We're like racing engines geared into nothing. We give off sparks and fire uselessly. There's nothing big enough to use ourselves on. We burn and go to waste and rebel and we have no cause. Rebels without a cause, that's us. Ah!" He stared at her wonderingly. "Look at you. You glow. Your eyes flash. You're a stunner!"

She blinked and laughed, then dropped her gaze away from the intensity of his eyes. She could feel a crawl of warmth in her cheeks. "I couldn't begin to be a stunner like you, Uncle Jack."

"Think I'm attractive, do you?"

"Of course. I always did."

"Then come closer. Sit on my lap."

She shook her head.

"Why not?"

She shrugged.

He moved across to the sofa she was on, sat beside her and put an arm around her shoulder. She tugged her skirt forward over her knees and sat rigidly.

56

"Scared of me? Think I'd do something wrong to you?"

"No. But—"

"Then why shouldn't we express the love we feel for each other? This bond between us is special, darling. I'm not just *an* uncle, but *the* uncle. . . . Right?"

She nodded, then giggled, her voice high-pitched. Flustered, she stood up. He got up, too. He lowered his face and pressed his mouth lightly to hers. At the touch she wound her arms around him, arched her body forward and mashed her mouth to his. Then she jabbed her tongue against his lips. He recoiled, his eyes widening. She hung on and giggled.

"You didn't know I knew how to kiss hot. Did you like it?"

"What the hell!"

"You get me excited, Uncle Jack," she said in a rush. "You always did. When I was real little all I'd have to do was rub against you or crawl on your lap to get all excited. Let's kiss some more. Kiss me like you did your other girls and your wives!"

He pulled her loose from him and, holding her firmly by one arm, marched her down to her own apartment.

"I'm phoning Iris about you tonight, Irina."

"If you do, I won't like you any more."

She slammed her door. Inside, she grinned nervously, then sobered, grinned again and sobered at once, the brief, swift expressions blurring, her feelings confused. Uncle Jack would never put up with her slamming the door in his face. She knew it fearfully and joyously at the same instant. She tilted her head, listening, waiting for his next move, her vivid eyes alert. She kept shifting her weight, lifting one sandaled foot and then the other very slowly, her legs gliding together, bare and warm under her cool, fresh, striped-cotton skirt.

After a few seconds of silence she heard Uncle Jack start to walk away. Her anger flared and exploded and she found herself in the hall glaring fiercely at his back. She stood with her legs apart, fists on hips, her thin neck and head angled forward, her mouth a small pink thrusting, her eyes burning at him like acetylene flame. He turned and stared darkly at her, feeling her challenge so strongly that his chin thrust forward and his mouth tightened into a colorless line.

The silence between them was like a tightening that

57

half-stopped her breath and made her heart beat faster. His eyes narrowed and seemed to recede like, she thought excitedly, fists drawing back just before striking.

He cleared his throat and said hoarsely, "You could murder me!"

She didn't answer but began to jiggle one knee so that her skirt pulsed with a frothy motion and made a whispery sound. For a split second his glance dropped to her skirt.

"Whether or not you like me, Irina, I am going to talk to your mother about you."

"That's final?"

She lifted her nose haughtily, turned and went to her open doorway. On the threshold she looked across her shoulder, thumbed her nose with one hand and with the other hiked her skirt up in back till her panties showed and swung her hip insolently toward him.

She started to walk on into the room. But he came so fast and his open palm hit her bottom with such cracking force that she fell forward off balance. An instant later she was hanging by the back of her belt from one of his fists while he spanked her. The belt broke and she fell and started to scramble and crawl away, but his arm hooked under her waist, hoisting her and he continued spanking. He got tired of that position and threw her on a couch face down. She lay there waving her legs, her fists beating the cushions while she said over and over in a cold voice, "You stop that. You stop that! I warn you, you *stop* it!"

"I'll *stop*," he said, hitting, "when you *beg*," he said grimly, spanking again to emphasize his words, "when you *apologize* . . . when you *promise* to be good . . . when you say you're *sorry!*"

"Please stop," she said. "I apologize. I promise to be good. I'm sorry."

He walked away. She lay there and began to rub her bottom. He walked back and ordered, "Pull your skirt down. You said what I told you to say like some parrot. There's not a tear in your eyes! I told you to *cover* yourself. D'you want some more?"

She lay with her face on one cheek, her eyes turned up into the corners toward him. She grinned, and covered herself.

"Not that hard, no."

He lit a cigarette, walked away and came back. He pulled up a chair to the head of the couch. She rolled onto her side, propped herself on an elbow and reached out and stroked his hand.

"Don't feel bad, Uncle Jack. I had it coming."

"I can't cope with you, Irina. I'll have to call your mother."

"I understand."

"If I could have some believable assurance from you that—"

Irina frowned thoughtfully. "I've changed my mind. I *want* you to tell her. You should. Yes, you should."

They looked at each other unhappily for a long while.

"I'll think about it," he said, and drew a long breath. He gave her a small kiss and left the room.

She knew he wouldn't phone her mother. And he didn't. Instead he initiated a disciplinary program. All her days were mapped out with a balance of fun, study, sober thinking about herself and regular consultations with him. She had responded to him and the picture of herself changed in her own mind. She obeyed him like a good daughter. Little by little she told him everything about herself.

There was a hectic interruption for several days when her parents came there and fought the final round in their marriage and agreed to end it. Noel and Elly went off to camps and she stayed put, and would be there till school.

By summer's end she was in love with Uncle Jack in a way she never had been. It was something untouched by excitements. There was just a lovely peace and warmth and understanding between them and the marvelous sense of great accomplishment. When she thought how he had just stopped his life and given it all to her that whole summer, she would want to hug him and kiss him. But when she did give way to that impulse, the physical contact made her nervous and she had a sense of fighting off something. She would have to get away before she got one of her mean streaks or became sexually stimulated.

Trusting him completely she told him honestly about these physical reactions to him. She had gotten over the idea she could be sexually exciting to him and ran around in sun suits, shorts or bathing suits, unself-conscious about her body. Especially in the easy, casual atmosphere of the lake cottage she felt free in his presence to sit or lie or sprawl however she chose.

Then one evening at the lake after a dinner with him at the hotel, they went back to the cottage. No one else was there. He had had a few drinks and was reading. She, too, was reading and thinking about the school year ahead and how well she'd do.

She was sitting semireclined on a porch chaise, her knees up, her skirt covering only the fronts of her upper legs and occasionally she'd open and close her knees. Uncle Jack was sitting in a position where he could by a slight shift of glance see the backs of her thighs clear up to her panties.

After a while she became aware that his glance was sliding off his book, that he was repeatedly looking at her intimately. Her heart began to beat quickly. She stretched her legs out flat, crossed her ankles. She'd put on toenail polish, not to be sexy, but because it made her feet prettier and now she became tinglingly conscious of that ornamentation. She got up and sat on a chair. She began to watch him furtively. He seemed absorbed in reading. She breathed a little easier and thought-hoped she had been imagining.

He poured himself a long, long drink of whisky and drank it down all in one gulp. Presently—she had the uneasy feeling she had to watch his every move—he went and stretched out on a lounge, sighing. He lay there for a while and when she glanced over he grinned and beckoned her with a forefinger.

"C'mere."

"I'd rather not right now, Uncle Jack."

"Ah, sweetie, I'm getting lonesome for you already. Just a couple more weeks and you'll be in that school. Gawd, I'll miss you. Aren't you going to be sad without me, too?"

"My gosh, yes, Uncle Jack," she said contritely. She hurried over to him and sat beside him and patted his cheek. She kissed his forehead. "I don't know how I'll live without you. Oh, you don't know how hard it'll be to be good without you there."

"You'll be fine. You've come a long way."

"But I've got an awful long way to go. Why, just a minute ago I was scared of you, imagining you were thinking sexy about me. I'm so ashamed," she said earnestly.

He drew her down and petted her. She lay stretched out beside him and she knew it was all right. And *then*. It was so smooth she didn't realize anything was happening. He turned on his side, face to face with her and put his hand on her bottom and patted and stroked and moved his body closer against hers. He had on trousers, but she could feel through them. He was in a man's state of excitement and when she tried to pull away he held her forcibly against him and began a rhythmic movement.

"Please don't, Uncle Jack," she gasped. "Let me go."

His hand was moving down to his trousers and she seized it to keep him from opening them.

"No. Don't . . . Oh, don't. *Don't!*" she begged.

"Shut up!"

He got agitated and grim. He was breathing fast and his face was flushed and his eyes were those of a stranger. Irina started to cry. He seized her wrist painfully and twisted her arm up her back, then he wrestled her other arm back of her and his big hand fastened like handcuffs to both her wrists. His other hand pulled her skirt up and she kicked and screamed and heaved her whole body.

She got one hand free and struck at him. She got loose and ran and he grabbed her and carried her bodily into the bedroom and threw her down on a bed and jumped on her like a wild animal and got his hips between her knees.

She lay beneath him clawing his shoulders and scooting herself frantically up the bed away from his lower body. She kneed him, rolled herself violently and fell off the bed.

She ran blindly and almost got out of the house. But he caught her. She saw he was exposed and it was terrifying. He threw her to the floor and held a hand over her mouth and bumped himself against her pelvis bruisingly. Then he seemed to have a horrible convulsion and something was happening, a fantastic, mystifying something.

Then all the wild-animalness went out of him and he crawled away from her. She scurried past him and got into her bedroom. She caught sight of herself in the mirror. She stared as if entranced with shock and disbelief. The front of her dress was wet and messy. Only then did she understand what had happened. She felt mingled nausea and relief that she hadn't actually been raped.

She changed her dress and then just sat on the bed,

sniffling and crying. He kept knocking at the door and talked through it. After a couple of hours she went out and faced him.

"Now I know why you were so nice," she said bitterly, "and didn't want to tell mother on me when I kissed you that time and admitted you got me sexy. You wouldn't have got a chance at me if she knew. And all this summer you just pretended to be making a good girl out of me. That's the last thing you want, for me to be good. That wouldn't be any fun."

"Don't hurl that in my teeth. I was sincere. But you undercut everything I was doing. You've never let up showing off those legs and swishing that fanny around and throwing yourself at me. Even telling me about all the sexy episodes in your life to try to arouse me every way you could! I guess you're proud—incurably, sluttishly proud of being able to do that to me!"

"*I* did that to *you?*" she cried. She stared at him, dumbfounded. "Oh, that's a good one. I never heard anything like that in my life." She stopped. "Yes, I did, at that! Miss Burkhardt said I seduced *her.*" She started laughing. "You know what, Uncle Jack?" She laughed harder. "You ought to have me arrested!" She screeched with laughter.

She was determined to tell her mother the next day. But Uncle Jack blackmailed her.

"When Iris hears the rotten underhand things you've done to her pet, Noel, and how you abused little sister . . . look out!"

"You'd betray a confidence like that, that I told you because I trusted you? You'd be that dirty?"

"I'd be crazy not to. If you got me in trouble."

She just stared at him venomously.

"No comeback?"

"I want you to know," she said passionately, "that as much as I loved you, I hate you. I just *hate* you."

"What a tart morsel you are. Give me a kiss, baby bitch."

She hopped back as if on springs.

"I told you I *hate* you!"

"If we're enemies, Irina," he taunted, "I'll have to talk. I'll have to include my version of how you tried to seduce me. Anything you'd say afterward would be marked down to spite and revenge—quite in character, y'know. We going to be friends?"

"Never."

"You know I wouldn't take your virginity and leave provable evidence, you cute little tidbit. You know you'll like it, you devil. And, you've got no choice."

"I can make a clean breast of everything to Mother."

"You won't . . . you won't."

"I'll run away!"

"But that would force my hand. I'd *have* to tell Iris. Better to have fun. Right, Irina?"

"Wrong!" she shouted. But it was a losing battle.

Every chance he got he had his fun with her, never penetrating, always leaving her, ironically, a technical virgin. Every bit of advance she'd made in her self-improvement went to hell. She got meaner and flightier and hated everybody, especially him. His power over her was vile and unbearable.

Sometimes, though, she thought with guilty excitement that hers was the superior power. A grown woman would have had to go all the way. But *she* had the unique allure to excite and satisfy his lusts without ever letting him really do anything. He never fully possessed *her*. And no man ever would! They would crave her and excite themselves and hurl themselves futilely at the gate and fall back exhausted, content just to strive for her even though she was forever unattainable.

chapter six

Larry seemed at first to be just one among many her mother dated before and after the divorce. Iris had been casually aware of him at various parties and functions for two years, but he existed in another circle, an acquaintance of acquaintances. For him she'd been a focus of interest. He recalled with flattering detail her regal coiffure at a certain dinner, her gown, jewels and slippers at a ball, her eye-compelling costume at a hunt breakfast. Accumulated desire gave his courtship a force that eliminated other suitors.

A get-acquainted-with-the-children period followed

when they did family-type things together, and one by one he had periods alone with each of them.

Noel and Elly were polite and wary, Irina impolite and wary. If, walking, his sleeve so much as brushed her arm, she gave him a warning look; if, talking about how he wanted to be friends, he smiled and gave her some compliment, she let him know she despised goo. She studied him furtively and became convinced he didn't really see her or anybody else but her mother.

About a week before the wedding he was standing alone out on a terrace and she walked past, saying as she went, "If you think it's because you're marrying my mother I don't like you, you're crazy."

She stopped a dozen paces away and began fiddling with some vines on a trellis. She watched him come. He stopped, not too near.

"Then why?" he said, baffled.

"If I liked you, you'd like me. Then I'd be nice to you, then everything would be ruined."

"Irina, I don't understand."

"I didn't ask you to. I don't want you to." She walked away again, into the house. When he didn't follow she turned and scowled at him, then went back out and stood facing him.

"You sneaked around and did something for me, didn't you? Mother told me you went up and saw the headmistress at Marleigh Hall and got me in there. Well, I won't be grateful and you'll be sorry you ever vouched for me."

"No, I won't. You'll make that school proud."

"Don't you know anything? Don't you know my record? Are you crazy to go out on a limb like that at a school where your sister and mother and aunt and even your grandmother went?"

"I know your record. I know what I'm doing. I know you, Irina, better than you imagine. I made a snap judgment about you the very first day."

"Snap judgment! I thought you were at least intelligent!" she snorted and left him.

She and Elly were flower girls at the wedding and she was required to wear a lavender dress, a big hat and a simpery smile. During the ceremony and later at the big reception on the lawn of the new house Larry presented to her mother, Irina tried to stay unimpressed by everything, especially him. If it were all just a show she was

64

watching, she'd enjoy the leading man's looks and like the protecting-something-fragile-and-precious way he acted toward the beautiful bride.

When the pair of them toasted one another, sipping from each other's glasses, they did it so charmingly she couldn't help smiling with pleasure. She decided to pretend it was a show that she could enjoy without being involved. Both he and her mother mistook it for a real acceptance of Larry. And maybe even then, that's what it had been. At any rate, she was soon won over completely.

It wasn't because of the tangible gifts and treats he provided, or because he occasionally talked to her on an adult level about himself. It was because he was what he was, because he rang absolutely true. And when he said she was his favorite, he was simply stating a fact for its own sake. He had no ulterior motive; he didn't expect any sly rewards. It was something he gave her as a free gift, the most priceless one she'd ever had.

As in everything, Larry was right that she would make good at Marleigh Hall School for Young Ladies. He willed her to succeed and she joined her will to his and the school itself was challenged. During the first two quarters of the first year she was under the closest possible supervision with private counseling three times a week. When in classes and study periods she was restless, she was loaded with additional assignments.

She finished the first year ranking in the first ten scholastically. In the second year she was at the top of her class and began to take on a proprietary air about the school and was appointed a Founder's Day Committee Hostess, a responsibility usually reserved to third- and fourth-year girls. She was an officer in three of her four clubs in the third year and additionally was elected by the nearby boys military academy as Color Guard Girl and then, at their Commencement, as Ball Queen.

She was elected president of the Theater Society, the Classics Club, the Marly-Gaters, and of her Senior Class. A student-faculty committee chose her for the elite Marleigh Honor Society. In addition—she didn't consider it ironical—she was an MBS (Marleigh Big Sister), serving as a trusted counselor to younger girls.

She had advanced, she felt, beyond the physical to the spiritual, from concern for herself to dedication to principles, from indulgences to sacrifice, from lust to love.

Love, pure love, was what she felt for Larry. On vacations at home and when he and her mother visited Marleigh Hall, she made her feelings clear.

The Marleigh Hall uniform, dark blue in winter, light gray in spring, consisted of three-button jacket, white blouse, straight, below-knee skirt, and moc-type shoe. Topping the ensemble was a smart beret featuring the school insignia on the wide headband. Stockings were utilitarian, underthings plain, including flannelette knee-length panties in the winter; sleepwear and washroom robes were prescribed without frills.

They were expected to be fastidiously clean, but ornaments beyond the school pin, merit and year stripes on the cuff, were out. Everything was calculated to distract attention from their bodies as specifically feminine; bath powder and light cologne were allowed but no other cosmetic or perfume. There was an official school belief, which she shared, that the glow of health and "the inner light" natural to a young girl were sufficient and that self-centered concern about allure was mentally unhealthful.

Marleigh Hall was within twenty miles of Cassmore Boys Academy and it was traditional for the girls to go en masse to watch the cadets' full dress parades, to cheer for Cassmore at football and basketball games and track meets. Smaller groups went to Cassmore every second month for a dance; in alternate months the cadets came to Marleigh Hall.

There were teas, picnics, exchange dinners in each other's dining halls, two annual formal dances. Sexless romance was encouraged in general, not specifically. Individual boys didn't invite special girls or vice versa. The schools extended invitations for a certain number of unnamed ladies or young gentlemen, and if too great interest was shown between a couple and they tried to monopolize one another, the privilege of such get-togethers would be withdrawn. The schools didn't try to discourage "natural affinities," merely seeing to it by vigilant chaperonage that these affinities were expressed in safe view of everybody.

Irina's particular affinity was Don Colby. A sandy-haired, very thin boy when she first knew him, he looked vulnerable, with his cap off, like a hungry baby—appealing and a little comical.

A year older and a grade ahead of her in school, he

had just been promoted to corporal, and though he considered himself above such petty achievement, he couldn't keep from fingering the chevrons. His ears were set unusually high on his head and the line from ear to eyebrow sloped downhill giving an impression of tilting his head forward with an air of great earnestness. His voice had changed and he exaggerated its depth and he took her, one of the smallest of the girls, to be terribly young and green and he decided instantly to be her protector.

On her next visit she was glad he was in the group waiting for their bus. She was next to last getting off. She could see him watching anxiously as girl after girl stepped off, and when she appeared he beamed and hurried to her and looked down at her so lovingly she wanted to hug him.

"Oh, boy, Irina, am I glad you got to come! How are you? You sure look nice today."

"You do, too, Don. I got to worrying on the ride that you might've got demerits and not be one of the boys."

"You did? You really worried? What do you say we think of each other as dates, even when we're circulating? I know personally there's not one girl in the bunch I'd rather be with. Will you do that, think you're my girl?"

"All right."

"I mean if any of the guys try to tell you how cute and all that you are, don't forget whose date you are."

"I won't, but bye-bye for right now."

He came to believe she was the finest girl alive, the most serious and idealistic and worthwhile. And as he rose in rank to sergeant, lieutenant and captain-adjutant in his final year, he became more certain that they were natural soulmates. He was aware that several of his classmates thought quite as highly of her and he was intensely jealous of her dancing with them or allowing them to fetch a cup of punch or offer to escort her to the buffet.

He was perpetually contriving to get her out of public view long enough to kiss her. She offered only her cheek, and he confirmed his opinion that she was of a purity unmatched by any girl since his mother. She really missed him when he graduated and went to college. He was still smitten and they exchanged letters regularly. He expected to marry her when he finished college and she more or less thought she'd accept him.

There was a phase when they wrote poetry for each

67

other. She produced odes to nature and to abstract virtues and was, on the whole, idealistic and impersonal. His were frank love poems of an exalted character, mostly concerning her merits of mind and soul and heart, and all the anatomical references were above her shoulders. When she wrote paeans to a male, she had Larry in mind, and he was just as bodiless in her poems as she was in Don Colby's.

Don invited her to a spring dance at his college, but she couldn't get permission to go, and wouldn't have even if she had been allowed to. She had too much on her mind. She had to keep up on school work and her functions as officer in several organizations and her job on the weekly paper and plans connected with commencement when she would be graduating *cum laude*. And there were two distressing personal problems.

First, during Christmas and spring vacations she had sensed a strain at home. However much Larry attempted to disguise it for the benefit of the children, there was a difference in his attitude to her mother. There was no longer the same convincing ardor in his eyes when he looked at her. Irina couldn't help thinking of the poem, *Ode on a Grecian Urn*.

The ideal situation in love was for the lover to be always in pursuit, never quite capturing the prize. Maybe the trouble was that Larry had captured her mother, and he no longer being unattainable had lessened her enchantment. Or maybe he felt she didn't give enough of herself to him exclusively. Her social calendar had always been full, and part of her original appeal was that she distributed her charm, wit and looks generously and flirted mildly as a matter of course.

Her mother hadn't needed to say anything in words. She had the anxious, somehow ruffled air of a woman who has fallen off her pedestal. She went to unusual lengths to cater to Larry. As proud as her mother was, this was astonishing and embarrassing. Usually her mother would have been coolly aware of herself and not made a spectacle of humility. It was clear that the tables had turned and that it was her mother who was the one most in love. Larry was too kind to relish such a situation. He tried to respond and be reassuring, but there was a definite rift.

During spring vacation her mother actually confided in

her that Larry had another woman somewhere and might ask for a divorce. Her mother's face had gone to pieces and she'd sat rocking herself in a state of desperation as helpless as a child. It had been heartbreaking.

Irina had gone to Larry, knowing she could talk to him about anything. But she'd become tongue-tied. He'd guessed what she wanted. He told her the subject was one he couldn't possibly discuss with her. She'd gone back to school leadenly, needing to do something, not knowing what she could do.

The second personal problem was at Marleigh Hall. Suji (Sue-Jean) Alton, an upper school girl a year younger than Irina and in the form below, had been seduced by Roy Portman, the math-geom teacher, just after Christmas vacation. Suji came to Irina and several other senior girls and tearfully confided everything. She swore them to secrecy, thinking she'd be disowned if her parents ever found out; besides she'd get expelled. She was actually wringing her hands.

After she'd left her unsolvable problem with them, they discussed it with disbelief and a growing indignation. There was little to be said for Suji's intelligence, personality of looks; she had no *"savior-faire"* and was, in fact, a blank. But dutifully, as Marleigh Hall girls, they liked her, and pointed out that she was obedient, not to say spiritless, cooperative and . . . well, she tried.

Roy Portman was the most attractive of the school's five male teachers. It was a bad year for him when fewer than a score of girls got crushes of him. He had only a store-window-dummy kind of good looks in Irina's eyes. His stock dropped sharply with the girls Suji confided in—they were contemptuous of his choice.

"He's deplorable," Mary Louise said. "Yet you could have a little respect for him if he'd had the taste and courage to shoot for a really terrific girl. Like Amy. Or Phillipa. Or you, Irina."

"Or you," Irina said with conviction.

"Thanks, darling. It's so unfathomable that a real man would prefer . . . I don't know how to put it. *You* know, Irina."

"Prefer dishwater to champagne," Irina said. "We're being vilely disloyal to Suji. We must love her; whatever flaws she has should make her that much more dear to us. I speak as your moral leader," she said, whooping with laughter. They laughed with her, then solemnly agreed she was right.

"Because Suji's weak and we're strong gives us an obligation. My stepfather calls it *noblesse oblige,*" Irina said gravely. "Now this poor girl has been abused. Many of us know how it feels coming back after vacation; we're depressed. That's how Suji was. Portman found her easy to handle in that condition. He took advantage of her when she was at a low point. He's branded himself a sneak, a bully, a yellow cur. If we begin thinking there's any possibility of admiring him if only he'd seduced a harder-to-get girl, then we're allowing our judgment to be swayed because he's a man. That's lust, not justice. The next thing you know we'll abandon Suji. Lust isn't just. How about that? Sharp? Lust isn't just!"

"But what can we *do?*"

That was a problem. They got Suji in the gym, exercised her to exhaustion; took her for endless hikes; fed her pills someone had heard about. And she had her period, for whatever reason.

Still, the fact she wasn't pregnant didn't end the situation. Shame and guilt began to corrode her. She had had only one thing, purity, and that was lost and she couldn't be reasoned out of the notion that loss of virginity damned her forever. They got tough with her and though she stopped talking stupidly, she began to act like a fool. She flaunted rules, went out of her way to get demerits.

Official lectures and punishments did no good. She was suspended. When she returned she smuggled in beer and cigarettes. They barely prevented her getting kicked out for good the first night back. Two nights later she went off limits and was expelled.

All the girls involved were unhappy; some of them cried. Each wrote a letter to Suji and showed it around to be admired by the others. Irina's masterpiece of consoling sweetnesses and encouraging platitudes drew exclamations of praise. They shone in one another's eyes as persons of lovely, proper sentiment, the sugar and cream of young womanhood.

Irina felt false. She continued to feel Suji's expulsion acutely. She began to brood and withdraw irritably. She wanted to tell the others that *she* was to blame. She knew they would reason her out of it and she remained silent.

Because somehow, she didn't know how, she *was* to blame.

She woke breathless one night, as if there were lead in her chest. The leaden sensation shifted from her chest into her upper abdomen, transforming into a seething, acid-like burning of anger.

For the first time her thoughts slashed at Marleigh Hall. It was a fraud; its sanctimonious pretense that girls had no bodies was hypocrisy. The obsessive denial of sex was a perversion that spread to their minds till the only right thinking was dishonest thinking that prettied everything up and concealed all the dirty truth about what they were.

She'd been dishonest. And because of that she'd let Suji get hurt, maybe emotionally injured for life. A closed-off part of her had understood Suji's problems better than any of them had. If she'd brought that hidden part of herself into play, she could have established a deeper bond with Suji and brought her safely through. But to have revealed such special knowledge would have shown everyone—herself most of all—that she was not really the wonderful person they all knew and believed in.

A thought of flashing intensity made her blink. Her vividly pretty little face became immobilized as she knew what she must do. A moment later her features squeezed together and she began to cry softly and forlornly because it was going to end, Marleigh Hall. And she didn't hate it. She loved it. She would die to be disgraced in the one place she had made good in. She didn't hate the false person she was; she loved her and she didn't want to be that other, terrible creature, but—she covered her face, sobbing aloud—she *had* to.

It was to have been a perfect thing, her record here. Year by year she had built and improved it. It was to have ended in the gloriousness of Commencement Week when they would come, Larry and her mother and Don Colby, and maybe even Noel and Elly.

They would see her as she was presented with three awards and four medals, and watch her receive the gold-tasseled *cum laude* diploma. They would see her proudly and know she was good and had become a person who deserved them . . . and . . . and . . . Now she wouldn't even graduate. Everything would be wiped out; every-

71

thing—even the future. She was going to bring back to life that terrible person she had been. She *must,* in order to do what she had to do.

The next night Irina called a secret meeting after lights out.

"Have you noticed," she whispered, "the disgusting carefree way Portman walks around? He thinks he got by with it. What kind of justice is it if he can get by with it?"

"It's terrible, but what can we do?"

"Expose him!" Irina hissed. "Get him fired!"

"We can't without hurting Suji. It would get back to her parents. They're such creeps they'd hate her. She swore if they found out she'd kill herself. She would, too; she's crazy."

"I know how to get him," Irina said. "Lead him on. Get him to make a pass. Get him to invite one of *us* over to the academic building after lights-out, like he did her. Only when he's there he'll be caught red-handed alone with a girl, and BANG . . . he's done!"

One of them whistled; others exclaimed enthusiastically.

"Yes, but—" Phillipa remembered. "The girl'd get it, too, for going there to meet him. She couldn't claim he came here into the upper school and stole her. BANG . . . she's done, too. And my gosh, this close to graduation. Our families are coming up for commencement; we've got dates for them, and all sorts of things we're involved in. Why, we can't do it. It's impossible."

"Not for me," Irina said. "I'm going to do it."

They protested that she had more to lose than any of them.

"I don't care," she said grimly. "I'm going to do it."

They began to counsel Irina on how to get him to notice her.

"That's no problem," she said indifferently. "I could have got him any time I wanted to from my first year on. I never looked up to him as if he was somebody who'd have to descend to notice me. Just the opposite; I see him as a flunky wishing he had the privilege of ascending to me. All Portman needs to believe is that he can get me and that I'm safe."

Roy Portman, a dark-haired man of medium height, in his late twenties, was in charge of the library during evening study period the next week. She arrived in the library near the end of the period Monday evening. It was warm and she wore no jacket, just a prim-collared, short-sleeved white blouse with the long straight light-gray uniform skirt.

At seventeen her back was straight, her stomach flat, her white skin taut, her flesh springily resilient. The uniform de-emphasized the ripening contours of her small, tight breasts and softly flaring hips. The skirt broke the continuity of the feminine curves from the narrow flare of her waist to her hips and ruined the superb lines of her long legs, but the natural charm and grace of her body in motion surmounted these handicaps.

She moved with assurance, carrying her head high on the stretched line of her neck and tilted a fraction of an inch to the left in an attitude of inquiry and insolence. At the time she wore her hair pertly in a short straight bob from which the lobes of her ears emerged pinkly. Her unusually pretty face was alertly responsive, lustrous; her startlingly colored eyes glimmered with animation. From the moment she entered the library to the time she reached Roy Portman at the central desk, she held his attention, though it was disguised, indirect.

She reached the desk and scratched her name on the register. He sat relaxedly and looked, though he was male and thin enough, like a smug, plump auntie. His face had no distinct, sharply defined features, but consisted of irresolute lines and planes loosely flowing together, because he didn't have anything inside.

No convictions, no character, she thought, loathing him. He became different things at different times and was only an uncentered creature of responses who shaped himself to other people and other situations, and between the commands of outside forces he just stayed inert.

When she finished registering and looked up at him he turned on his shallow, "warm, friendly" smile. Ordinarily she gave him a cool, indifferent smile.

Now, though, she initiated her plan. She disdained such obvious devices as contriving to show her legs, leaving off her bra, swishing or flirting. She believed she could stand in a crate with only her head exposed and rouse a male to heat just by looking at him. She would convey the sexual allure of her whole body with her face alone.

She looked at him quietly and steadily for six or seven

seconds and without any perceptible change of expression she simply stripped her face naked, and let him look. The force and heat of her wiped off his tepid smile. He blinked, straightened uncomfortably on his chair. He did not, he could not, look away until she released him. She turned herself off and went casually over to the little spiral staircase and walked up. En route she saw he was watching her, baffled and *hooked*.

She chose a study booth on the balcony and sat in profile to the open iron railing and looked at a book. She seemed unaware of him below, glancing up at her time and again. He got up and strolled the lower floor, posing as usual for some of the girls down there who watched him adoringly. Now and then he smiled down on one of them, but he kept sneaking looks up at Irina every chance he got.

He was, she guessed cynically, looking for an opening —for an off-guard or deliberate, careless or calculated, shift of her body around in her chair, a relaxed separation of her knees. It wasn't an unknown practice, and for all she knew, half the girls on the balcony line were providing views of knee rounds or pale, shadowy inner thigh. She showed him nothing.

Once she turned her head slowly, gazed across her shoulder, her face again "naked," as she thought of it. Something was lost in the distance, but not too much, not too much. *Flunky,* Irina thought, *sneak, coward, cur.* She hated him with a fullness she had never known, because it involved not just her uncontrolled emotions, but her total mind, too.

She ignored the end-of-period buzzer. She sat as though totally absorbed while everyone else filed out of the library, a few stopping to check out books or exchange words with the "god."

When they were alone, he busied himself with routine at the desk, pretending not to know she was still up there. Finally he looked up.

"Miss Devereaux!" he exclaimed. "I thought you'd neglected to check out, but you're still here. It's past closing."

"Oh, my goodness. So soon! I don't suppose," she said hesitantly, "I could have a few more minutes?"

"Well, I've some finishing up to do. It's all right."

74

"Thank you."

Presently he was checking stacks and study alcoves on the balcony. He looked in on her in passing and she gave him a quick, sweet smile. When he came back and said, "About finished?" she shut her book and stood up.

"Of course you know," she said in a hushed voice, looking down and smoothing her skirt, "I heard the buzzer." She looked up slowly, showing her "naked" face.

"No." He shook his head. His face colored slightly. He cleared his throat. "I had no idea."

"You supposed I was too studiously absorbed to notice anything?"

"Naturally. A student of your rank. An honor society girl . . ."

"Model of propriety? Scrupulously correct? Exemplary young lady?" she said silkily. *"Virgin?"* She grinned.

"Miss Devereaux! I'm—" he groped for the word—"shocked." She continued to grin at him. He suddenly laughed. "I'd never have suspected you had the slightest interest in me."

"Because I never flirted? That's little girl stuff. False advertising. I'm only interested in real experiences. I'm circumspect. I'm smart. I stay under wraps."

"That you do, Miss Devereaux!"

"Irina, Roy. You're my type. Mature. Commanding. I used to think college boys were men. But they're too young. It's difficult to find them discreet at that age. Not content to enjoy, they want to boast. I know you'd be cool enough to keep your mouth shut in case—well, we'd better break it up for now. See you tomorrow night. Maybe we can get more definite."

She spoke quickly and started past him into the aisle. He caught her around the waist and tried to kiss her. The thought of his sickening mouth on hers was nauseating. She evaded him, raised her eyebrows and said wearily, "Anybody could walk in that door down there, any minute. If we get caught in a clinch we're in trouble . . . and for what? Let's save the preliminaries for the time they lead to something. . . . G'night, Mr. Portman."

"Good night, Miss Devereaux."

She had casual public encounters with him next day in a hall, on a walk to the dining room, coming out of chapel after vespers, strolling at twilight on the upper-middle school mall before evening study period. She presented the familiar picture of self-sufficiency, involved exclusively with school affairs and other girls.

Her competence at deceit would lull him and establish a sneak's bond between them, she thought, or else he would believe she'd dropped the whole idea. In fact, she did abandon it for a few minutes out on the mall that twilight. The five-minute bell sounded, calling them in for study period and she found herself in an emotional state.

She stood out there on the lawn, looking from a little distance at the large, squarish upper school building with the dull yellow sunset light warm on the lacework of climbing ivy that covered the dark stone and fringed the rows of windows. She absorbed it into herself like a time exposure on a photographic plate, holding her eyes open till they smarted. There was a drowsy-sweet feeling in her flesh as when drifting into or out of sleep.

She remembered a story about a person who had taken root and become a tree and wished she could bury her feet in this place and remain forever. She moved reluctantly toward the building, trying not to jar the delicate and exquisite sense of peace within. She moved lingeringly to the little porch and through the open double doors into the cool, old-wood-smelling lower hall as though into an embrace of goodness, strong and solid and safe. Her eyes filmed and her breast ached with a sense of profound loss. She could not, could not for any reason, betray this place, this thing, this person that she truly was . . . wasn't . . . was . . . wasn't . . . was. . . .

She was privileged to use her room instead of study hall for evening study. Her roommate was gone. She just sat alone in the sanctuary, staring at nothing and thought about the deep-down abusive, vile things she had done, and she saw Elly's whimpering face and Noel's anxious eyes and Suji's anguish, and most of all her mother's distressed face. She must make the sacrifice. Must lose all she'd gained. Must die to be truly reborn. Must suffer punishments for her own sins. Only in that way would everything be made right: Suji avenged, Larry and her mother brought back together. It was *commanded,* somehow. There was no choice. Nonetheless she could not rouse herself to go to the library that night.

She regathered her strength and will the next day and near the end of the study period she went in the library.

Not showing up the night before had worked to her advantage.

"I thought you'd changed your mind," Roy said, when they were alone, his tone petulant, like a small boy with hurt feelings reproaching mama.

"I wanted you to have time to decide if I'd be worth a little risk," she said matter-of-factly. She took a folded sheet of paper from her loose-leaf. "Here's a copy of the watchman's schedule last month. His rounds begin from various places and on no two nights does he reach the academic building at the same time. If there's a regular pattern, it would take a man's mind to discover it. Maybe you can figure it out if—" she looked at him levelly—"you're interested."

"I'll look it over and . . . Where're you *going* so soon?"

"I've a meeting before lights out. Uh. . ." She frowned at him. "I'm assuming you'll protect me. I figure to celebrate Christmas in nine months, not Mother's Day. Okay? . . . Seeing you."

He'd done his homework next night.

"The pattern's easy. There're only seven variations. Each night of the week is different. But the same route every week. I'm surprised you couldn't figure that out, Irina."

She shrugged. "You've done the brainwork. How about the action?"

"I was thinking . . . ah . . . the English class room upstairs in the Academic Building. It's the full width of the building, windows on both sides and in the end wall so that we could see anyone approaching from three directions. You could get there from your building through the vestibule without going outside. I can enter at the far end of the building. How's that sound?"

She nodded slowly. "So much for where. When?"

"Say one night next week. A week from tonight. Between the watchman's twelve-ten and one-ten rounds. We could meet five minutes after he left the building; leave five minutes before he returned." He blinked and watched her, almost holding his breath. "How about it?"

She looked at him coolly.

"How about tonight?"

"Well . . ." He took a slow breath and nibbled his lower lip. Confronted with a right-nowness, he started tippy-toeing around in his mind. He glanced at her, away

77

again. She watched him steadily, with rising tension, wondering if he suspected a trap.

"Cluck-cluck-cluck," she imitated a chicken very softly.

"It would mean breaking a date," he said snappishly. "And for what? Maybe a joke. I haven't had so much as a kiss to show you're not just . . ."

She rolled her eyes, let out an exasperated breath. She glanced at the open door downstairs, then moved out of view behind a stack.

He followed and she turned her face up. She received his kiss with tight, puckered lips, then unexpectedly she opened and began to flick the hot tip of her tongue against his mouth. His arms tightened around her. He began to deep-kiss her. She gave the slightest little roll to her pelvis, grinding softly against him. She could feel his male response like a leap of sudden life. She pushed him away, watched his agitation amusedly. He grinned shakily.

"No fooling around about you," he said admiringly.

"Tonight?" she asked composedly.

"You know!"

By ten o'clock "lights out" everything was set. Five minutes after she left for the tryst, her roommate would go down, wake the housemistress and report Irina's absence along with suspicion of where she was and why. Within ten minutes they should get to the Academic Building.

Irina undressed and went to bed as usual, expecting to lie awake. But at a quarter to twelve she was being gently wakened. Three or four girls in robes and pajamas were sitting on the sides of her bed, another two or three were hovering out in the room. She was helped up and into her robe, and petted and given whispered endearments.

They surrounded and embraced and kissed her, one by one, and told her what a heroine she was, what a martyr. They began to get tearful and the mood began to penetrate her and she became frightfully emotional and overwrought and started to cry, too. They gathered round to comfort her, and in the hushed commotion one of them lost control and cried out aloud. They hushed her. Everyone became dead silent, motionless, listening.

"Look!" someone hissed. From Irina's second-floor corner room they could see the swinging lantern of the

78

watchman on the walk going from the Administration Building across to the far end of the Academic Building. He vanished and they waited . . . and waited. . . . After an eternity they heard him come out of the Academic Building into the vestibule. He came outside then and along the walk under the window, his keys tinkling, the lantern beam spraying against their building briefly.

"Well," Irina whispered, "I might as well start." She drew a long breath.

"Don't! Oh, Irina, *please* don't go."

"It's all set." Irina looked at her roommate. "Honey, you be *sure* to get the housemistress. Raise a ruckus! Get her over there. I can't stall him off very long. If anything should *happen* to me, I'd . . . Well, it just mustn't. I'm saving myself for Don Colby. I'm practically engaged to him. Don't fail me!"

"I promise. I'd never let you down, Irina. But, oh, I'm so scared for you. You're so brave I could cry."

"Well, don't. And don't anybody else. Everybody get back to her room. Please . . . G'bye-bye," she said to one after another in parting embraces. "I'll miss you so! I'll never forget you. Any of you . . . my best friends . . . Good-bye."

They were all gone. She listened till they were in their rooms. She went out quickly and down to the main floor. It was empty. She went down a half-flight to a landing where the door led into the vestibule.

She slipped outside, moved rapidly across to the Academic Building, eased open the main door and stepped inside. She adjusted her eyes to the heavy darkness, and began a cautious ascent of the main staircase. The wood creaked, and she stopped on the main floor, just listening for any other movement within the empty building. Then she hurried up to the second floor, feeling unaccountably giddy.

She had every reason to feel anxious, but she wasn't in the least frightened going down the long, dark hall. She reached the English room and peered through the upper pane of glass before going in. She didn't see anything but windows and the lines of movable one-arm classroom chairs. She went on in to wait for him. Moments later a figure came out of a shadowy corner toward her. She caught her breath and her heart jumped into her throat. It was Roy Portman.

"My God, you scared me. Why were you skulking there? You scared me to death! You! . . . You!" she cried angrily.

"I had to know it was you," he said tightly. He attempted to embrace her at once. She pulled his hands away and felt his fingers, cold-tipped. "Are your feet cold, too? Calm down. Take it easy. There's plenty of time."

She went to the little desk platform and hoisted herself into a sitting position on the desk. He followed, caught her face in his hands and kissed her hard. He withdrew, then at once kissed her again. She got her head free, wiped her mouth.

"Don't be greedy. Don't be wet."

She pushed him and he went back like a blown feather. Not, of course, from the force of her shove. He moved with swift, near-silent purposefulness to the front line of student chairs and began to undress. His actions were blurred, obscured in the dark, but she saw his shirt was off. Then his trousers.

Good! she thought. He couldn't have any explanation for that. She sat on the desk, ankles crossing, knees pressing together, her spine and neck becoming tense. He was skinning his undershirt up and off. Then—her chest lifted on a half-breath and stopped—he was fingering the waist of his shorts, unbuttoning them.

In the dark he was a dangerous night creature. She lowered herself almost motionlessly off the desk, felt the tips of her slippers touch. She'd go in the hall and hang onto the doorknob and hold him trapped for the minute —the maybe ten minutes—it would take for help to get here.

She ran for the door, her arms half-lifted, winglike. He seized them from behind and spun her around. He was stark naked and looming over her and she could smell his body and his heat. His hands were at her belt, then the lapels of her robe. He unpeeled it from her like a sausage skin.

"No more playing, no more teasing," he said in a warning half-grumble, half-whisper. "No more hiding it. You hot little piece. . . . Stand *still!*"

She'd kept stumbling back and he'd kept in contact. He had her against the wall, unbuttoning her pajama tops. He touched her skin. He squeezed her bare breasts. He yanked the tie cord of her pajama pants. They fell away from her stomach and hips and clenched buttocks, but her locked legs held them up.

He caught her under the arms, lifted her whole body and when she kicked at him the pants and one slipper fell off. He carried her to the middle of the room. He kept hold of one arm, crouched and spread her robe on the floor. He pulled her over to stand on it. He paused to regard her exquisite nudity and said on a slow exhalation of breath, "How about that!"

Her body was luminous in the dimness. Light stroked her shoulders, the upper slopes of her jutting conical breasts and her belly, hips and rounded buttocks; shadows cupped under her breasts and pooled in her navel.

Her figure had the graceful lines of a fine vase. She saw his dark-glowing eyes follow the taper from her hips to the slenderness of her ankles and felt his hot-palmed caress on her smooth, cool hip. She recoiled, taking a mincing, half-step backward. She had a giddy-gleeful sense of her beauty and power, power for good.

He was all animal body, she was mind and spirit; he was feverish, she was controlled. She would command the pace, she knew, as he began to kiss her throat and shoulders and breasts, his mouth like a wet dishrag. His lusting hands moved on her bare skin excitedly, but unexciting.

He tried to pull her down, and himself went to his knees, his head below her breasts. She could have spat in his face and trampled him under her feet. He swooped her legs out from under her, laying her on her back, and he lay half on his side, his nakedness against her. She kept her intimacy resolutely shielded against his touch with both her hands. She estimated that the housemistress was now awake, now on her way. It was only a matter of minutes until this loathsome creature would be exposed for the thing he was. He was prying more insistently at her hands.

"The protector!" she said sharply. "I told you that!" She sat up.

"It's all right. Lay down." He pushed her down. "Take your hands away. . . ."

She held tight, reinforcing her position with crossed legs. He got her hands away. His urgent, prying hands were manipulating her. She rolled and squirmed and momentarily pushed the hand away but it came back like a creature at her throat. Then he made the discovery.

"You're a virgin! You liar!"

"Yes. Let me go. I was just playing!"

"Damned teaser. You're going to *get* it!"

She lurched, hit, scratched, rolled.

"Don't you dare," she gasped. "Don't you dare rape me."

He subdued her.

"I won't rape you," he said grittily.

He held her and began to caress her with almost savage insistence. Trying, she knew, to create sensation and response and consent. She stayed icily unresponsive. It was easy; she loathed him. She would hold to her purpose and integrity and superiority.

She tensed against a sudden flick of sensation, painful, hateful sensation. It flicked again . . . and again . . . quick-darting as a serpent tongue. It was intimate and— she shuddered—pleasurable! She felt a hot, sweaty flush over the skin of her whole body.

Then the heat focused into flicking little delights of intimacy which abruptly expanded into twitchings and throbbings within and she could feel a gauzy slackening of tension in her limbs. She wanted to scream, to smash him to death. But the rushing, fierce momentum of desire, of wild craving, was sweeping away her will, and she hated, hated, hated with all her force at the same time that she was beginning to submit, and she wanted to die.

Everything began to swirl. She thought she'd explode with ecstasy. And she *was* exploding helplessly. But abruptly he wasn't there. He was on his feet, crouched, tense, listening. Steps were coming along the hall.

He was in wild motion, trying to get into his clothes. But the door opened. Light flooded the room, catching him half undressed. The housemistress, her assistant, the watchman, gun drawn, came in and stood in gaping silence.

Irina sat up, pulling the robe around her. She looked at Roy Portman and the anguish and terror of his suddenly bloodless, shiny-wet-eyed face touched her with unexpected pity. A trapped, helpless animal.

Swiftly, as she realized she'd come through unpossessed, her feeling changed. She was glad she'd punished him, glad she'd ended his career here. She'd destroyed him, she thought exultantly, and gave him a look of gloating malevolence. The bitchy side of virtuous action had its satisfactions too, she thought, then rejected the thought at once. She covered her face, crying, as the housemistress looked at her and began to speak in a grim, outraged voice. . . .

Larry and her mother met her train the next afternoon. Larry spoke in a casual voice and smiled. Her mother embraced her limply, forced a smile and on the ride home kept her mouth shut with visible effort, as if she were going along with some idea of Larry's and not her own decision.

"You may freshen up and rest in your room, Irina," her mother said at home. "You may remain there during dinner . . . or you may join us. As you choose."

Larry walked up to her room with her. He put an arm across her shoulder and squeezed lightly. "We'd *like* your company at dinner. It won't be a lecture period. I promise."

She did go down to dinner in a pretty cotton frock, and Larry, fresh and bronzed and solidly handsome, kept the conversation going with a flair and ease that struck her anew with wonder. Most of the time she was looking with wondering, loving eyes at his end of the table, responding girlishly, laughingly, to the warm amiable mood he was creating for her. She ate with fine appetite and had two desserts, which greatly annoyed her mother, who ate almost nothing and smoked six cigarettes and had trouble keeping the flint out of her eyes when Irina looked at her.

For coffees and liqueurs they went onto the terrace which sat at the top of a fine slope of lawn with the lovely pond below. Irina exclaimed gaily over the view. Larry went to the liquor cart and she stood opposite him. Her mother paced to the end of the terrace.

"Larry, might I have a liqueur? I'm old enough." She gave him a sweet-girl, round-eyed and adoring look that made him chuckle.

"Well . . ." He hesitated, glancing toward his wife.

"She's certainly old enough," her mother said edgily. "From what I hear from Marleigh Hall!"

"Iris, we agreed. . ." Larry began.

Her mother flung herself irritably on a settee. "Lovely, lovely. How long's this pretense to go on? Have your liqueurs, you charming people. . . . By *God,* Irina, you little *slut!*" she shrilled suddenly.

"You haven't heard my side!" Irina flared. "It's true I was found with that creature with my clothes off. But I'm still a virgin. I *planned* to be caught. Or, if, as forever, Mother, you would rather believe the worst about me, all right. Thank God there's at least one person in my life who tries to understand and wants to believe nice things about me."

She went to Larry and hugged him. She walked to her mother. "You want to hear?"

"Of course I do. What can you mean, you planned to be caught?"

She told them about Suji, told them why she had had to bring justice to Roy Portman. They questioned her repeatedly throughout her account. At the end they seemed dazed but convinced.

Her mother went into the house, came back out with fresh cigarettes, lighted one and began to pace, shaking her head more and more impatiently.

"Oh, Irina, what's wrong with you? You never have any sense. I thought you'd got past that phase of total all-out involvement. Do you always have to go hog-wild? Nothing short of destruction will do? Couldn't you have punished the man with concerted scorn? You girls couldn't have given him the silent treatment, for instance?"

"We thought of that. But the reason behind it would have come out. Somebody would've blabbed. Suji's folks would have found out eventually."

"Oh, what of it!" Her mother made a slashing gesture. "You've got enough to handle handling Irina. What did you accomplish for the girl? Tell me. Nothing! And look what you've done to yourself! And me. For God's sake, Irina; you've driven me crazy all your damned life. . . . Well," she retreated, "I shouldn't have said that. I know you tried, baby. You were doing so damned well, honey. You *shouldn't* have done that to yourself. Not for any reason, Irina, not for *anybody's* sake!"

"This may not be my business," Larry began.

"Don't be silly. You're more a father to her than her own ever was. She feels that."

"I do absolutely, Larry. You've got every authority," Irina declared, gazing at him with brimming eyes. "Punish me any way you want!"

"No punishment. Far from it. Iris, what you're over-looking is the meaning of this kid's action. I tell you it's a beautiful thing she's done. This is an example of pure altruism. She's sacrificed herself for the sake of someone else. And she knew what she was doing. She lost all she'd earned at that school by doing it. She *gave* everything she valued. And I take off my hat to this girl."

"I see it," her mother said. "It hurts me. I don't care. I don't want her hurt. But you're right, Larry. We should be proud. And, Irina, we are. Honestly."

She rushed into her mother's arms, crying and hugging her.

When they separated Irina raised her face and said, "There was more, more to it. I had the feeling of making a propitiatory offering to the gods, somehow. I felt exalted. I felt that I was not just avenging poor little Suji, but saving something far more precious." She looked at Larry. She looked at her mother.

"I was worried more about your marriage. If it broke up I didn't know what I'd do. I had to do some big, good, hurting thing. I had to sacrifice. That way . . . Well, I thought everything would be right . . . good . . . paid for . . . you'd stay together and be happy. . . . Do you see?"

They nodded. They stared at her with a kind of awe. Then they looked at each other uneasily. They thought she was crazy. . . .

The truth was, crazy or not, the marriage became stronger after that. The sight of her mother belonging fully to Larry again gave her the greatest satisfaction—for a while. Then she wasn't so sure she wanted her mother, or any other woman, to have Larry.

chapter seven

After the phone talk with Larry she slept most of the day she returned from Reno. She dressed and had dinner in a quiet neighborhood restaurant on West Portal, then drove out to the ocean and cruised slowly along the Great Highway. She found a parking place remote from the various clusters of cars along the uninviting beach and just sat watching the ocean in a sort of torpor until about ten.

A squad car stopped and the officers lectured her. She was agreeable, even docile, but they kept looking at her oddly. When she started her car and drove home, they followed her all the way.

In the apartment the phone was ringing; she wanted no dates or parties or any contacts with anybody on a personal basis and she didn't answer. She brought typewriter, paper, pens, notebooks and books out to the table in the dinette corner of the big sitting room. She partially opened the pair of casement windows within the expanse of the big picture window so that the steady fresh west wind off the ocean flowed through and out the kitchen. She got into pajamas and robe and switched on a TV news program and made herself coffee and ignored another phone ring.

She switched off the TV and lamp and stood in the dark staring out the window and sipping coffee. After a while she settled down to study for her 10, 11:30 and 2 o'clock classes next day, listening, as she worked, to the distant sound of the sea and the nearer sound of a softly tuned all-night radio music program. She fell asleep in a curl on the sofa at four o'clock and was up early, feeling fresh, crackling with vitality.

After classes she went to the Stonestown shopping center grocery and bought food enough for a week. Stocking her refrigerator and kitchen shelves gave her a settled domestic feeling.

Larry's special delivery letter came late in the afternoon. She slit it, ran over and sat tailor-fashion by the big window, nervous with expectancy. It was on his business stationery: LAWRENCE CAVANAUGH AULT AND ASSOCIATES, but handwritten in Larry's blocky script:

Irina dear:
    I write this immediately after our phone talk and you should have it, air mail-special delivery, tomorrow afternoon. Your emotional state worries me. It recalls the unstable child I first knew. We both sensed, as you became a woman, that our bond grew stronger, that our paths, instead of diverging naturally, tended to join. Unstated, we knew instinctively that a break was necessary.
    I let you attend college so far from home to encourage

86

your freedom. You've resisted this independence, Irina. There has been an accusation against me in your manner sometimes, Irina, as though I had withdrawn my love and cast you out. I must have your assurance that you understand me better than that, and that you understand yourself.

Don't phone! Think. Then write. To the office.

Love as always,

Larry

Irina read the letter twice, slowly and carefully then rushed to her typewriter to compose a reply:

Dearest Larry:

Destroy this. I understand you. I understand me. We had to put distance between ourselves. Or the finest thing in my life would have become guilty. I'm not an innocent any more, Larry, in any sense. But the guilty things I do must never touch you.

When I'm with a wild crowd I am the wildest. I seem unable to bear, or to resist, overstimulations. I shall live as quietly in these remaining college weeks as if I were still a Marleigh Hall Honor Society Girl, which, really, Larry, I always am in my heart.

How many, many times you've reminded me that there *is* a tomorrow. How many, many times I allow myself to forget it and to be taken over by a rushing dark feeling as if I am blind and running wildly away from—toward—*something*, and that the next step, the very next step, will be the void, the drop-off into some kind of nameless destruction. Oh, I don't know why I said that. You'll think I'm in a dreadful state. But no, I am calm.

The apartment is quiet and I look out across a small and lovely lake and beyond that lies the Pacific like an endless sheet of fire in the sunset. And close by I see a coastal freighter gliding south and in the distance the diminishing dot of an Orient-bound ship. And if a phone should ring I would let it ring for I have detached myself from a wrong group and from parties and I am looking forward to many, many tomorrows.

I am going to write a letter to Don Colby and enclose a copy for you, so that you will be assured that I reach out for a future separate from you—though never too far, h'm? Believe me, Larry, just that. And keep yourself well. And tell Mother that you love her, please. Tell Noel I have heard how well he is doing in your firm and that I'm happy about it and about his marriage. I want to know when Elly has her baby; she doesn't write me. I want everybody at my Commencement.

What more is there? I could write on and on and never stop, for they hold me to you, to you all, these words do. I'm going to be fine. I sign this with love, I sign it, your
Irina. Always.

Dear Corporal Colby:

I saw a Marleigh Hall girl last month who had seen you on Wall Street with a mustache and the air of a coming young man and a dispatch case lettered Siler, Colby, Evans, Colby and Perdell. She guessed you were one of those partnership Colbys, you fake. But imagine you with a mustache; imagine me with a bachelor girl apartment in San Francisco and living it up and getting nostalgic for my first love, Don dear.

I went right down to Montgomery Street and looked in on the local branch of your firm, and I almost told everybody I knew you. Knew? Know? What ho?

Sentimentally,

Irina.

Always.

She went out to mail the letters and came right back. She had a leisurely shower and put on silver-cloth lounging pajamas and matching slippers, and combed her hair back two sections, tied at the ends with frisky white ribbons and felt young, sweet and virtuous. She walked about incessantly, her step soundless and light on the carpet, the legs of her pajamas whispering wordlessly.

She was stimulated, not overstimulated. The inner feeling wasn't a seething rushing, but a slowness like the fermentation of fine wine. When the phone rang, she finally answered in a soft-singing voice. She swayed her head away from the angry, high-pitched female voice.

"I want to speak to Phil Harkness right this minute!" It was June Earlson.

"He isn't here, June," Irina said gently.

"You're lying! I know he came there. I know he did. You'll be sorry, you'll be sorry. . . ." The phone banged.

The phone rang five times in fifteen minutes. The gang was back from Reno and they wanted to have a little blow-off. With an easy graciousness she deflected their insistence on coming there, rejected invitations to go out anywhere else.

"I'm sorry . . . I'm sorry . . . Playtime's over."

"Whom am I speaking to whom?" Jim corned. "At least I gotta return your skis and poles."

"No hurry, dear. Thanks so much."

Jim came twenty minutes later and he came alone. To get the skis and poles inside it was necessary to unchain the door, and he slipped in, uninvited, and swung the door shut and leered down at her in a way that made her scalp crawl. A feathery sensation ran the length of her spine and it occurred to her that virtue was easiest practiced in a vacuum. She moved out of his reach.

"I'd rather you go, Jim."

"Not even a drink to reward the faithful servant?"

"Esther wouldn't like it, our having a drink together alone here. I'll see you on campus tomorrow. Do go."

She walked across the room toward the big window.

Clouds on the horizon rose from the sea like mountains of fire cut by purple and black ravines. The reddish-orange light was like blown embers. It mirrored on surfaces of her pajamas, rippling and running like flame. The moving flamelight caught and held Jim's gaze and drew his body. She paused and stood profiled by the window so that one side of her glowed and the other hovered in shadow.

Jim came and faced her and looked at the glossed gold and silver mounds of her breasts. He stood there half-lighted, half-shadowed. He was transformed, not the safely-engaged-in-love Jim she had known.

He kept looking at her, a sort of thrust about his whole face, the lips and eyebrows bunching, the nose tightening along the flanges so that the tip seemed to sharpen.

"Let's cut this out," Irina said softly.

"I haven't touched you," he said almost inaudibly. Then he joked in a hoarse, solemn tone. "No thankee-kissee?"

"Just one. If you promise no handy-panky."

He came a half-step forward and she lifted her upper body slightly, bringing into clearer definition the mounds of her breasts and compressed her lips into a diminutive, succulent mound.

His lips settled on hers lightly, then heavily, as if he were trying to sink right through her. His hands came up and spanned her waist and slid under to her bare flesh, moist and hot. She pushed his chest, but he drew her lower body to him and began to breathe fast and clutch her bruisingly.

She weaved her head from side to side, but his head

kept coming down like a pecking chicken, scattering kisses all over her face and throat and the triangle of bare skin just below her throat. He tried to tug her like a sack to the couch.

"Stop it," she said in an icy voice. Almost at once there was a hard, quick knocking on the door.

"Christ, if that's Esther!" Jim whispered.

"Get in the bedroom," she hissed and pushed him. "Get going!"

He moved and she followed, pushing repeatedly. When he was inside Irina had a confused swirl of giddy-guilty-gleeful feelings. She grinned at the prospect of facing Esther, who had always felt so smug and safe and superior about Jim. She went to the door, swung the metal cover away from the peephole. She stared through the little circular opening and her heart literally jumped with joy.

It was Suji. Sue-Jean Alton from Marleigh Hall; older, fuller in the face, rather prettier. Dear Suji, she thought, groping to get the door open, a living testament to her virtue, come to express her gratitude for what she had done for her. Irina swung the door wide to welcome the dear living proof of . . . of . . .

It wasn't Suji, of course. It was June Earlson, plump, face flushed, blond hair stringy. She'd been crying, but now she had an hysterical courage and she shouted past Irina, "Phil Harkness! If you don't come out of there this minute I'll—"

"He's not here," Irina said quietly. "Calm down."

"I want to see. You've got him." Tears began to gush. She wiped at them and her mouth quivered. She swallowed and stared wide-eyed. "Let me look!"

"Come in." Irina stepped aside. June rushed through the sitting room, into and out of the kitchen, back to Irina at the hall-closet door.

"There!" June stabbed a finger toward the shut bedroom door. "I want to look in there."

"I won't let you." Irina took a fist-on-hips stance, blocking the door. "He's not there."

"He is!"

"He's not."

June shut her eyes and rushed at Irina, who calmly rammed her with the heels of both hands with enough force to knock her down. She sat there stunned, looking up at Irina. Then she scrambled up, ran out into the hall

90

and down the fire escape door. Irina looked out, then abruptly sprinted. June was opening the door, going out. Irina caught her by the coat on the little landing outside.

"What're you up to?"

"I'll kill myself."

"Oh. That again." Irina released her coat. "And your wrists still bandaged from the Reno razor job. A jump this time, h'm?"

"I'm no good. I never was any good," she said, panting, her eyes wild. "I know. I never was. Don't try to stop me. I don't want to live."

Irina watched her move over to the railing. June half-sat on it, stared at Irina, now out of reach. June looked over the side, seven floors down to concrete.

"Well, June," Irina said casually, "you're not too bright and you have little character. Your kind of prettiness doesn't last. It's the bone structure. In another few years you wouldn't even have prettiness. And if you say you're no good, you've probably got reasons. You know your true self better than anyone."

"I do! And don't try to stop me, because I'm going to jump. Tell Phil good-bye when you go back to bed with him."

"You want to go in that bedroom and see he's not there?"

"Oh, by now, sure, he got out."

Irina shrugged, didn't deny it.

"That's true, isn't it?" June demanded.

"No," Irina said lightly. "I'm going inside now, June. I'm not your judge. If you've inspected yourself and found an inner rottenness—"

"I have!"

"—then who am I to interfere with your self-imposed death sentence?"

The two of them just stared at each other. June hovered on one haunch on the narrow iron railing. She kicked off one shoe, then the other.

"You think I haven't got the courage, don't you, Irina Devereaux?"

Irina said nothing. She watched the rabbit trying to become a lion. Subtly, very subtly, not quite like stepping over there and pushing her, Irina's mouth began to curl slightly, expressing a depthless scorn.

Irina felt her heartbeat quicken sharply. Her senses

91

dizzied. She watched June with brilliant, unblinking eyes. June gave a sharp cry and started to swing her legs over the side. Irina stood locked, motionless, thinking, *What a kick, what a bang, what a sweet, unique, ice-cold thrill!* watching somebody's last few seconds of life, seeing it and feeling it close-up. . . . Her head ached. She was brittle. There'd never been anything like this, it was marvelous. Did June have the guts? Did *she,* Irina? Not quite . . . not quite . . .

She snapped herself into action, rushing and grabbing June around the waist. She pulled her to safety. She almost dragged her into the building and back to the apartment.

"Jim," she shouted, "come out and show yourself!"

Unresisting, June allowed them to pour a drink into her.

"Phil wasn't here, hasn't been, doesn't intend to be," Irina assured her. "He doesn't want me. I threw it at him so hard he couldn't stop. It wasn't your fault, June. But this suicidal thing with you, June! You'd better get unkinked."

They located Phil after making a few phone calls and he came and took June in hand.

When Irina was alone she knew all her own plans were changed. To hell with college and promises and everything but claiming her rightful man.

Twenty hours later a dealer had bought her furniture, to be picked up next day; an expressman had carried out the things she was shipping; her suitcases were at the door, packed; she was dressed for travel. She would drive, not fly. She wasn't frantic to become Larry Ault's mistress; she already was, and had been from the moment she'd decided to be.

When Irina Devereaux set a goal, she reached it; her decision to do a thing was inseparable from the thing done. *Her wish be fulfilled,* she thought, *her will be done.* it was as inevitable as the appearance of light when she turned the switch. Smiling, she flipped the switch on-off three times in succession. She carried her suitcases down and out to the Jaguar and in minutes she was en route.

chapter eight

Crossing the country Irina maintained a fast, steady road speed and drove long hours. But she got her sleep, exercised regularly and watched her diet because she must arrive glowing. She toyed with bizarre ways of making her presence known to Larry, working out details of time and place for maximum shock effect, but discarded them all.

Early Sunday afternoon she reached the turnpike cut-off within twenty-five miles of home and checked into a motel. She stretched out on the bed and rested for three hours, alternating between sleep and a kind of voluptuous torpor. When she got up and showered and changed clothes, she looked sparklingly fresh.

And she felt that way, driving the final miles. At sight of the big house on the hill with lights showing on the main floor everything in her quickened. The yellow-glowing gatepost and lane lights were on, and she switched off her headlights and followed the climbing, curving lane to the top. She parked beside four guest cars and walked back to the kitchen entrance. She went in, putting a hasty finger to her lips as an unfamiliar maid gave her a wide-eyed, caught-breath look.

"I'm Irina," she whispered. "I want to surprise them. Who's here and where are they?"

"In the little dining room. There's the mister and your mother. You brother and his wife. Your sister and her husband. Then there's—"

"Plenty. Plenty. Thanks."

She left the kitchen, detoured through halls and rooms, crossed the big dining room to the doorway into the family dining room. She emerged behind her mother's chair at the end of the twelve-place table. She tiptoed in, holding up a silencing hand as the others saw her.

Larry, heartbreakingly handsome in a fawn jacket and maroon shirt, sat facing her directly from the far end of the table. He raised his broad, strong, healthily tanned face and saw her! He started visibly. His eyes fairly

93

popped! She gave him an arch grin and wink, and a smile, like a sigh of pleasure, spread slowly across his face. Conversation came to a stop.

Irina stood close behind her mother's chair and leaned slightly forward till her chin almost touched the crown of her head. She gazed straight toward Larry, her face a younger replica of, and above, her mother's, showing him something, stating something. Her mother was almost at once aware of her presence and before she could sort out her reactions Irina snowed her under with effusions and embraces.

Irina made her way down the table pausing to cheek-peck and belly-pat pregnant Elly, to hug Noel, to smile at the others. Before going to Larry she slung her car coat on a chair by the wall, took off her silk head scarf, and deftly fingered her hair, achieving a certain mussed-up piquancy. She was wearing a dark pleated skirt, a wide, shiny red belt that nipped her waist sharply, and a clinging snow-white sweater.

"And now for Big Daddy," she cried gaily.

She went to him with a feeling of exuberance that gave a light strut to her step and swung her skirt enticingly around her lifting knees and made her thrusting breasts jiggle.

It was nakedly obvious that she wore no bra, and Larry, turning his head as she stopped beside his chair, saw and tried not to see at the same time. She embraced his cheeks in both her hands, stroking delicately. The feel of his dear flesh against her palms and fingers made her hunch her shoulders. She studied him solemnly, then bent and touched her lips to his forehead.

"Are you glad to see me?"

"Of course, of course," he said, a trifle nervously.

With a lithe turn and swing she seated herself across his lap, laced her fingers behind his neck and gazed into his face, totally absorbed, her back to everyone else. Then, deliciously, with everyone watching and seeing nothing, she stripped her face naked and let him see her. At the same time, so that he could not misread her expression, she imperceptibly tightened and relaxed her buttocks and thighs, a single, sensual pulsing of her flesh against his legs. She could feel the run of tension through his powerful muscles. He looked past her.

"Noel," he said calmly, "would you get Irina a chair?"

"Sure thing, Larry."

Irina stood up. Noel brought the chair. Irina placed it beside Larry's and sat down. Noel reseated himself and looked at her critically.

Irina looked at him and said casually, "Almost everybody who sees Noel remarks what a good-looking boy he is. Ten, twenty, thirty years from now they'll be saying the same thing. Good-looking boy."

"Now, now, Irina!" Larry said mildly. "Hungry?"

"Not," she said softly, "for food." One of his hands lay on his lap. She put her hand in his and held it, squeezing lightly. "What did you say, Mother?" she called.

"I said, 'No explanation why you're here?' No letter, telegram, phone call. You just airily walk in and settle down and don't offer a word."

The grim tone of voice and strained lines of her broadening face did little for her endearing, not-so-young-any-more charms, Irina observed.

"My reason is love." Irina nestled her fingers more snugly between Larry's and squeezed lightly and repeatedly. "Love's a woman's law. You always said it. I obey it. Finally. I began to ask myself what meaning a college degree would have and if I needed one and if I could spare the time it required and if, considering the importance of the love in my life, I wasn't endangering my future by remaining on the West Coast. As Napoleon was saying the other century, geography is history. If I'm there and my would-be husband is here, geography's against me; somebody else could make history with him and—"

"Would-be husband? Who in the world?"

"Don Colby. I've known him since my first year at Marleigh Hall. Remember him? He was here only a couple of summer's ago for a week. Stayed here at the house. Larry remembers, don't you?"

"I think so, yes."

"Nice chap," Noel said in the pompous way he affected. "Cassmore Academy."

"Of course!" Irina's mother's eyes brightened. "Don Colby. Nice family. Money of his own. Still, he was a bit callow and young."

"We all age, mother," Irina said cryptically. "He's older now. I'd characterize him less as callow than idealistic. I suppose his nicest trait is he never fell out of love with me. Nonetheless, girls around here might exploit the proximity bit. Proximity," she added with a glance and half-smile at Larry, "is a very great factor. I don't want to keep risking my future by not being on the scene with the mostest. So, if everybody would like to get on with the more important business of eating. . ."

The meal continued but some of the coziness went out of it, she observed with satisfaction. When the party regrouped in the game rooms in the basement, Irina got help and took her things to her rooms, which had included Elly's rooms for years. She left her door open, half-expecting her mother to appear. Sure enough, she came.

Without preliminaries she began to talk. Irina had anticipated that her mother, being a woman of formidable will and alert instincts, would be upset by her arrival and try to discourage her from living there. But far from seeing her as a rival she looked on her as an ally! And what she'd come for was to ask her to seduce Larry—in a nice, nonsexual way, of course.

"I've so often thought about and appreciated you, Irina. That schoolgirl sacrifice of yourself you made hoping to save my marriage!" she said wistfully. "You've guessed that he continued his ways. Right now he spends three and four nights a week in the city. The girls don't last but there's a succession of them. I keep thinking they're never what he really wants. Just substitutes."

For me, Irina thought.

"For daughters he doesn't have," her mother said. "He's very paternal. What he first loved in me, I think, was a childish quality he imagined. He saw me as a butterfly, flitting and innocent-eyed, seeing the world new and fresh. A butterfly with wings of steel," she added drily. "I was formed, my character complete; there was nothing basically he could shape or influence. I love that wish in him to mold and improve and create. I really love him for everything he is. And the stronger my feeling, the weaker my hold on him.

"I need reinforcements, Irina. Elly can't help me; she's wrapped up in the coming baby and she's too loyal to her own father to give Larry any real love, you know. You're the one with him. Now that you're here, if you could make him feel you still think he's wonderful, if you showed you enjoyed having him around, if you didn't overemphasize your Don Colby . . . well, it could be nice. He'd stay home more, center his life on our friends out here. I'd be able to walk around among my friends with—oh, more confidence. They laugh behind my back!" she said, with sudden bitterness. She paused, her eyes pained. "Well, you see, I need you, Irina. The time's come when I have to have some help."

"I'll do what I can do, Mother. . . ."

When her mother left, Irina smiled to herself. *I'll keep him home, all right!*

She didn't rejoin the party. She unpacked, then she busied herself in an aimless-seeming but vital routine of re-establishing physical connection with and ownership of everything in her rooms. She lay on the beds, sat in the chairs, touched desk, tables, bureaus, dressers, walls, drapes. She crouched beside her record collection, scanned her library, inspected her clothes storage closet, her bathrooms. She opened the French doors and stood on her balcony. She rearranged things, planned changes. She repeatedly darted looks at herself in the mirrors. Before long she had the firm sense that she was not only back, but had never really been away.

All the while she listened for signs that the party was breaking up, that the intruders were leaving. Then it was happening. She stood listening to the good-byes, counted one . . . two . . . three . . . four departing cars, Noel and his wife last. The servants had retired to their rooms and apartments in the big house and over the garage. Now there were only the three of them. The Master, a feudal lord at heart, who knew his sexual rights to every female within his domain . . . the Dame, a hollow shell holding only the illusion of power . . . and the true Mistress!

Irina partially opened the door into the hall. She swung her lounge chair around to face the French doors to her balcony. She slipped her shoes off and arranged herself comfortably, semireclined. She simply waited, not even willing him to come, knowing he could not help himself from coming. Soon afterward he was on the steps leading up from the second floor. He was in the hall. He was rapping lightly.

"Asleep?" he said quietly.

"No."

"Dressed?"

"Yes. Come in."

He came across the room and stood beside her.

"Iris asked me to look in and find out if you want a snack. Or a nightcap. And if you're all right."

She didn't answer. She sat looking down along her body. She mustn't look up, mustn't shift his attention to her face and diminish his awareness of her body in that submissive posture.

"Are you all right?" Larry repeated.

She felt breathlessly aware of his towering, overpowering male presence. She lifted her head and continued its motion backward with a dreamy slowness to the headrest. She lay looking up at him, eyelids half-closed, lips half-open. Her gaze went to his hand, then shifted meaningfully to her proffered breasts, lifting on an intake of breath, soft-mounded and stiff-nippled under the white sweater.

"Touch me," she whispered.

His hand hung motionless, his far-above-her, god-solemn face refused, and he spoke deep-voiced and calmly quiet.

"Irina, in my letter I told you—"

"That," she interrupted, "you've been as tempted all along as I've always been. You pointed out that I'd run away across the country. Well, I've come back."

He retreated a step, shaking his head. Irina sat up, thrust her face compellingly up at him.

"You're *glad,* Larry. Look! Your hand's begun to tremble," she whispered. "Touch me! Don't fight against it!"

He made a militant half-turn, and fairly marched to the door. She leaped up, sprinting past him and spun around, facing him. She teetered on the balls of her feet and spoke in a husky undertone.

"Who's running away now? I came back to accept it. I love you. I say it. I love you. I repeat it. I love you. I belong to you. My mind, my heart, my body.Everything!"

"Quiet!"

He clutched her shoulders and shook her. "You're very disturbed. You don't realize—"

"Don't lecture a child. This is a woman. A passionate woman! I'm going to love you, Larry, the way no other woman in the world ever could. It's all been a lie. All these years you've worn a mask, a protector's, father's mask. So you could possess me in an *innocent* way. But

98

you know your true self didn't want it innocent. You were *afraid. I* was afraid! Not now! Not any more."

"Calm down, calm down!"

"And put on the false front again? No. It's perverted me. Fixated me on you, made me crazy with unfulfillment. I can't love any other man! As hard as I've tried, I can't. I won't go on this way. You've *got* to claim me. Or . . . or . . . I'll do things! They'll put me away in an asylum. Do you want that to happen to me? Larry!"

"Your mother's coming up," he warned.

"Her! You know what she begged me to do? Play on your paternalism to keep you from sleeping out."

"You don't mean it, Irina."

"She did! Anthing to keep up the appearance she's holding you. So her friends won't laugh." She laughed silently. "Come to me tonight, Larry," she said in an undertone, then walked calmly into the hall as her mother reached the top of the stairs. She smiled winningly.

"Guess what, Mother! I convinced this mean man that I *wasn't* crazy to quit school in favor of love. And tomorrow night he and I are going to have one of those old time talk-fests about my favorite subject. Me. And my future. I promised him a special dinner menu, though, so you'll have to tell the cook I'm in charge. Will do?"

"Silly . . . of course! Are you settled all right? Is there anything special you need?"

"No. I'm right at home. And very happy to be here."

They had retired to the master bedroom a timeless time ago—an hour? Two? She wasn't sure. She'd bathed and creamed her body and perfumed it and she waited, knowing he would soon be moving through the silent house, to come to her, to claim her.

He didn't come and he didn't come. She remembered a dance she'd done last summer at a raffish drunken party, and the costume she'd worn and the music she'd danced to. She rushed to her record library, made a swift search, located the record. She prowled through her stored clothes and found the costume. She put it on and the black silk robe that went with it, finally the high-heeled bare-back sandals. She stood thinking intensely—oh, yes, there'd been another touch of voluptuousness! Fur! She got two fur coats out of sealed bags.

She hurried out with the coats and the record and

down the stairs, her heels ticking lightly. She went clear to the basement game rooms, past bridge table, ping-pong area, to a cushioned lounge area with a vast stone fireplace, record player, TV and a small, polished dance floor. She spread the coats on the floor, fur side up. She put the record on and toned the volume down and played it three times, letting it whisper into her, not dancing, just remembering the feel of the motion in her body and the mood, the fiery, wanton mood. . . .

She climbed back up to the third floor and went in her rooms thinking Larry would be there. He was not. She set her jaw. She stood frozenly, remembering when she was fourteen and had sneaked into the master bedroom in a shorty nightgown. She had had to know, then, that she wasn't out of her mind and imagining Larry. She had gone and he had not touched her body, only her face, and he had assured her she was his favorite! She would go now and release him from his prison of virtue and he could give her a man's proof that she was his favorite! She drew a long breath and smiled. Her smile was shaky.

She went out, just as before. And down just as before, and reached the door, just as before, and feared to turn the knob, but turned it. She entered and fused her senses with the dark and with the sleeping figures. She did not so much walk as drift like shadow to the beds.

Her mother, a trivial fetal curl in her bed, was masked, ear-plugged and further benumbed by pills. She did not stir. Irina stood beside Larry's bed. His hand was outflung, and she touched it, and it gathered around her hand startlingly. He was awake. But guiltily he didn't say a word. She pulled lightly and he sat up. He got up and put on slippers and a robe. They both moved out into the hall. When she smiled up at him, he said gruffly, "We're going to *talk*."

"Downstairs," she whispered.

She went to the basement in a rushing silence with Larry following closely. He truly imagined, she thought excitedly, that they were going to *talk*. She darted ahead. She was standing at the record player when he came in.

"You have to see what I meant," she said breathlessly, "when I said in my letter that I'm the wildest when I'm with a wild crowd. It's a me you've been unable to imagine, Larry. . . . Sit down. Sit down. Just observe

100

me. How can you talk out a problem without knowing what it really is?"

For minutes he fought a word battle he wanted to lose. At last he settled in a chair and she set the record spinning and turned up the volume slightly. She walked over and, kicking off the sandals, stepped onto the fur coats. She stood for a moment bodiless, the black silk robe covering her slim, sexy body from throat to instep, her black hair a loose shoulder-length frame for the excitement-flavored, off-beat beauty of her stark-white face. Her intense, vivid eyes were wide and her smile softly provocative when she dropped the robe, exposing her pale bare body, stunning in a tiny bikini set dazzlingly with chip diamonds.

She posed, elongating its graceful lines with arms lifted overhead, one knee bent to give her hips a sexier tilt. She could feel the record's music flowing sensually over her. A clarinet gave a long-drawn, quivering wail eloquent with lust and a feverish spasm caught at the fingers of a bongo drummer. Irina turned herself slowly, relishing the sensual friction of expensive fur under her naked feet.

The tiny upper band of the diamond-studded black satin bikini rode light as a stripe across the intimate points of her impudently thrusting breasts. The narrow triangle below clung to the soft, shallow underslope of her belly like a glittering arrowhead. Lacework at the sides bared the white-satiny flare of her hips and the seat panel was snugly styled to cover without concealing the pertness of her high-rounded bottom. She watched Larry watching her, tight resistance compressing his features.

A drummer with padded sticks set up a beat on the kettle drum and a trumpet sounded a series of high notes like swift tongues of raw flame. Other horns and a piano came in. Irina, suddenly taut and angular, picked up the primitive beat with her hips. Her little midsection swung from side to side, jutting one hip, then the other, her body gliding bonelessly with the horns and stopping abruptly on the commanding beat of the drum.

She began to lift her feet and sleek legs with quick-strutting grace and to stomp with light precision, sending little tremors along her soft inner thighs. Her pelvis circled and jolted; her torso undulated voluptuously; she caressed herself sinuously, her long black hair brushing her white shoulders.

The naked beauty of her flesh and the hot-flashing dazzle of jewels winking from her enticing derriere began to penetrate Larry. She teased her fingers repeatedly at the hip ties of the bikini.

The tempo of the music increased and her flushed body quickened to the compelling beat. Her dance grew wilder, approaching a state of abandonment. The beat, the primitive, jungle beat-beat-beat, lashing her, driving her, carrying her helplessly. Then silence, like a crash! The music stopped, its fiery pulse continued in her flesh.

She stood on the balls of her feet, legs spread, knees bent slightly; her mouth panting and open, her eyes riveted upon Larry. He was staring, his eyes transfixed. He had come erect, his upper body leaning toward her. His breathing was deep, lifting his powerful chest high. A suffusion of blood deepened the color of his face, and she saw the pounding in his neck arteries.

If he restrained himself another instant, she thought wildly, his head would burst, blood would flow scarlet over his whole chest. He was not restraining himself. He stood and without shifting his eyes from her for a single instant he took off his silver-gray robe and pajama top and then he dropped the trousers.

He was naked, thrustingly, commandingly, splendidly naked, and he came toward her, his neck arching. She could not resist the overpowering desire to reach out and touch him intimately. She felt a wild spasm of pleasure run through her whole body. Then he was kissing her mouth with a fervor and force of desire that made her limp.

She thought she was going to faint. He was picking her up. He was carrying her. He put her on the wide, long, cushioned lounge and she lay on her back, exultantly surrendered to him. He quickly removed her bikini, pausing to kiss and caress as he uncovered her.

Then she was lying naked, knees raised. He was saddling her buttocks in his strong hands and lifting her and she shivered and fit herself to him, wrapping her warm legs to his hot body. Then he was in intimate contact.

The touch was like a stab of heat that sent a violent, shuddering thrill into her flesh and she began to throb. He began to possess her and she cried aloud with joy, then briefly with pain, for he was powerfully built.

The rhythmic beat was in them both and there was

no pacing to his love-making, no slow period, no quickening and intensifying of the rhythm. It all seemed to take place in a final stage and something like a series of explosions seemed to be going off in her continuously, and she scarcely knew when it was done or when it began, for it was one unbroken state of ecstasy. . . .

When, afterward, he was lying beside her embracing her so closely that she seemed part of his heated flesh, she could feel the force of his slamming heart and the lighter, quicker throbbing of her own heart. Some of her dizziness cleared.

She half-said, half-moaned, "Oh . . . oh . . . dearest . . . lover! What a man! What a magnificent lover!" She kissed his throat, hotly, wetly. She clutched him harder against her flesh.

"Are you happy?"

"I've never been so happy. I love you more than ever. Say you love me."

"I love you. I love you so much I don't know how I've lived without you!"

"You'll never have to again."

They just lay filling themselves with each other for a long, measurelessly blissful time. At last they went upstairs. She could not part from him. She begged him to go to her room. They lay together again on her bed and soon she craved him again. She began to caress him and he roused and kissed her ravenously. And again he covered her and satisfied her deeply.

"I never knew what a man, a real man, could be. I never knew a man before and I'll never again, Larry . . . it's forever and ever!" she told him just before he reached the peak of pleasure.

They were both seized by the furious, rising, irresistible rhythm. Their bodies tensed, thrusting together in the final moments. Then she enjoyed a sweet, exquisite release. And from the depths of him came the life substance of his virile body given to her body, a gift, an offering, a draining of his power, and she smiled with love. And with triumph.

103

chapter nine

It was a time, that spring and summer, of secret delights and hidden thrills. The sense of violating taboos, the feel of conspiracy running in a dark, strong undercurrent between them, the piquant awareness of constant risk, quickened even the most commonplace things with excitement.

Even Don Colby, essentially still a dull, regimented boy soldier, though appealing in a bland-sweet way, took on interest in that atmosphere. He was like, Irina had giggled to Larry in bed, a sleepwalker approaching a cliff.

His answer to her letter was forwarded from San Francisco. It began, "Dear Color Guard Girl and Ball Queen," closed, "Faithfully, Cadet Captain-Adjutant Colby," and was full of boyish whimsies and remembrances of things past that never had actually been.

He idealized the glimpses of her he had caught during a certain phase when she herself had been a sleepwalker. Two summers ago, during his visit here, she had tried to give him another, truer picture of her. She'd expressed tart attitudes and sophistications which had made him laugh admiringly. He'd always considered her witty and he supposed her sharp new way of seeing things was a matter of mere words, somehow unconnected with the ideal soul. She'd thought his conception of her was a little touching, rather sweet. And she was very gentle in her efforts to prove to him that she had a body, that she desired to be made love to.

They had gone down to the float on the pond one night that summer two years ago, he in swim trunks, she in a skirted, dressmaker swimsuit. They had lain on their backs in the dark, holding hands and looking at the stars, and the feeling of being together had been as soft and lovely as the light-stroking balmy air on their bodies.

There had been a sense of richness in her, a profoundly sentimental feeling for him as her first love. She had thought she still loved him, or if not him, something about

104

him, some innocence, or defenselessness or clean-sweet something. An overpoweringly tender impulse, as of surging maternalism, had possessed her and she'd sat up and made a lap of her legs and asked him to rest his head there.

When he had done it, she sat stroking his face, dipping now and then to kiss his lips or chin or forehead, and he had purred with pleasure. Then she'd wanted to be held and had sat across his legs and they had kissed on the lips, passionlessly, lingeringly. His hands had stroked her arms and her shoulders and upper back.His fingers ventured a few inches down her chest toward the neckline of her swimsuit, then he'd withdrawn.

"You may touch me, Don," she whispered. "Anywhere."

She had coaxed his hand to the material covering her breasts. He had touched her hesitantly. Then she had shrugged off a shoulder strap and urged him to cup her bare breasts. And while he pressed the sensitive flesh she kissed him, not passionately but warmly. She drew back and gazed solemnly into his eyes. "Do you like feeling my breasts, darling?"

"Yes . . . Yes, very much," He said. He fondled her savoringly. "But—" he began, then was silent.

"But what?" she urged.

"It . . . it makes me. . ."

"What?"

"Desire you."

She glided her cheek against his. "It makes me desire you, too," she whispered. It was true, truer every minute. "Very much. . . This would be a lovely place. I've saved myself for you, Don. A lot of men have tried to make love to me. I always stopped them from going too far. Because I wanted *you* to be the first! I knew you wanted it that way. I won't stop *you,* sweetheart. I want to make you happy. . . ."

It had been true. She'd saved herself for him. She'd been his for the taking. He had not taken. He had covered her breasts and he had dived into the pool and come up wet, cold and smug with virtue (and fear he might have to marry her before he was ready).

She didn't see him again till after her sudden return from San Francisco. After reading his forwarded letter she phoned him and invited herself to lunch in the city next day.

They'd met in a busy midtown hotel lobby. The dark blond mustache was neat, and in his narrow-shoulder charcoal suit, button-down collar, narrow-brimmed hat, he was attractive enough, but he was strange to her. Because, somehow, he was strange to himself. The boyish earnestness had become a pinched look around the eyes. His bustling air, unnatural to his tempo, was tense, not vital. Unorganized crowds hurrying in all directions had the feel of goalless, meaningless chaos for him, he later admitted.

When he reached her and smiled down, his pleasure was unmistakable, but she had the odd insight that almost anybody familiar would have had the same soothing effect, made him feel secure.

Since then she'd seen him regularly, having lunch and sometimes dinner in the city with him almost every week. Occasionally she stayed in for a show and a night club afterward, then remained overnight—in a hotel and alone, she had to assure Larry, who was not as jealousy-proof as he liked to believe!

Don always got her to his apartment for a drink and to make a dutiful pass, and she effortlessly disentangled herself. He always felt better after the effort—it was a kind of embarrassed assertion of manhood and apology for his past refusal.

Taking her to her hotel after one such successfully unsuccessful attempt, he nestled her to him and said contentedly, "I'm sure we'll both be happy that we've kept our heads, Irina."

"Don, are you a virgin?"

"Of course not. After all!" he laughed. "In the past two years I've had ten—no, eleven—girls. One at a time." He laughed again. "These weren't girls I intended to marry. They knew it. It was all right with them. I felt no compunction. But with the girl I plan to *marry* . . . well, we're both going to be happy we restrained ourselves."

"I didn't say yes to you."

"You will."

"I would have, two years ago," Irina said. "Meantime, I've been engaged five times. I'm no virgin."

"You're not?" he said, emptily. "You're *not? . . .* Well

106

. . . I let you go. It's my fault. I thought . . . well, I . . ." He looked unhappily down at her. "You gave yourself to . . . you thought you were in love with and submitted to . . . who? Who was it?"

She sat away from him stiffly. "To somebody. In the dark. In a fraternity house. There were couples all over the place, on chairs, floor, couches. Everybody was drunk. I was necking with a man. He got up to go after a drink. He came back—only it wasn't him. I didn't know it. He didn't know who I was." She grinned. "Funny thing. Next day this fellow who'd had me thought he'd deflowered *his* girl and he proposed to her and she yelled yes, *fast!* He didn't find out till they were married and in bed the first night." She suddenly laughed. "Imagine his consternation finding out she was a virgin. The story got all over the campus. It was a scream! He never did find out who the mystery girl was!"

"What a dreadful experience for you, Irina! And to think . . . to think that *I* . . . yes, *I* was to blame. When my intentions were—"

"Oh, hell! Forget it. Now, if you're still interested in me, stop the nauseating purity-girl thinking about me!"

"Your mother has invited me for the weekend again, Irina. I'm coming. And I'm going to keep asking you to marry me!"

Don came almost every weekend. He became a familiar to the family, friends, friends of friends, the country club set. He dined with them at the club and at the inn favored by her mother's crowd, accompanied them to parties at other homes, took on a co-host air when they were entertaining. Socially he was pleasant and courteous; he didn't drink too much, swam well, was moderately skilled at physical games, and an amiable —too amiable—loser. She'd whack the ping-pong table with the paddle and order, "Come take your beating," and he'd come eagerly and finish beaten and grinning.

At word games he was slow, in charades he was un-inventive, but excelled in deferences and compliments, paticularly to older women. They liked his eager-earnest appearance and high-set ears and vaguely courtly manner toward his little sweetheart.

In a white jacket on a dance floor with her, moving placidly with a certain air of formality, he looked nice;

his stripling height set off Irina's petite figure and she wore fresh, dainty pastel frocks of young-charm simplicity rather than sophistication.

They were not only a picture couple on such occasions, but a picture family. Irina gleefully imagined what the onlookers saw and thought. The pretty little Devereaux girl's mother and doting stepfather watched the young lovers with unusual interest. How cute the way the girl would flirt and coax her stepdaddy onto the dance floor.

Dancing with and snuggling happily against Larry right out in public, Irina would giggle softly and say: "Everybody thinks it's just darling how I get around you, how you can't refuse me anything."

"I can't."

"The way you watch to see he's not packing me in too tight against him! As well a daddy should!"

"You devil!"

"Don's impressed by how well I get along with a stepfather. I told him, 'Oh, yes, we're very close. He puts me to bed every night.' "

Larry chuckled.

"Everybody's seeing how I can make you laugh, what a great big happy family we are. H'm . . . look, mother's smiling at us—a kind of hope-it-isn't-so smile with a soupçon of sick-at-the-stomachness, wouldn't you say? Wave to her to show you remember her."

"Honey, you're rough!"

"I bet you had your eye on me when you married her!"

"You were only thirteen, sweetheart."

"Mohammed married a six-year-old. And remember the Balzac novel where the man raises a little girl to be his mistress? Besides, I was only fourteen when a man got so steamy he couldn't hold back!"

"What? Who?"

"Oh, somebody. I'd never tell you—except if it would excite you."

"I don't like to hear about you that way!"

"All right. All right, lover. At the end of this dance I'm going to think you're so darling that I can't resist giving you a great big kiss smack on the mouth—a *French kiss.*" She laughed.

She did it, too. And everybody thought it enchanting —with the possible exception of Don and her mother. Driving home, Irina sat with her official suitor.

108

Occasionally it was obscure just whose suitor he was. Don was genuinely taken with her mother and it showed in the way he listened and looked when she spoke, in his tone of voice with her. He found her young figure astonishing, her face even more beautiful in some ways —more mature—than Irina's. Iris had that certain extra something that he could only define as "well, authority. . . ."

His admiration flattered her mother. In the wake of one of his Sunday night departures—lingering, reluctant for him, since he hated going back to the "rat race"—her mother had said dreamily, "He truly cares for me, that boy."

"Mother, he's a growth-stock type. The prospect of my looking like you twenty-odd years later makes him feel I'm a good buy. He's got a mother complex—like," she added with delicate nastiness, "Noel."

Her mother got her back up.

"Leave Noel alone. And there's nothing wrong with Don Colby. You treat him despicably. Like a dog."

"He begs for it," Larry said casually.

"Whatever she does is right. Right, Larry?"

"It really isn't our business how she treats him. You're not going to marry the boy . . . I hope." He laughed.

"Don't be funny. Irina, you're sadistic."

"Masochists bring out those things," Irina said.

For a moment her mother just stared, grimly.

"Specifically, Irina, you wait till Don's at the far end of a room or patio or pool or wherever, and settled in a group, enjoying himself. Then you summon—that's the only word, *summon*—him in an imperious tone and make him come trotting. You had him on his knees putting your sandals on you, like . . . like a *flunky*. You don't care one damn for him."

"Because I'm naturally dominant and he's submissive to me?" Irina asked airily. "Well, it seems I inherited not only a figure and face, but bossiness. That's where I get my high-tailedness."

"Don't speak to me in that tone."

"Whenever you're big enough you rule. The same with me."

"You don't love him. It's a farce, this romance."

"If I want to put a leash on him and walk him around at my heels, I'll do it If I want to make him lick my feet

109

in public, I'll do it. You hate that, not because he's being humiliated, but because I'm wielding power. Well, I love in my own style."

"A woman in love is submissive."

"I lack spinelessness. I inherit *that* from you. When you were in your prime—" She paused and let the word sink in—"everybody said how you walked around like you were balancing the Declaration of Independence on your head. Well, I walk that way, too. When you're strong, you rule; when you're weak, you're ruled."

"Oh, you're submissive enough in other relationships!" her mother lashed. She looked scathingly at Larry, then back at Irina.

"What do you mean?" Irina demanded, lifting her chin. "If you're comparing my relationship to Larry, the man I look up to as a father—if you're comparing my feelings for him to those connected with a would-be *husband* . . . well! It's vile! Do . . . you . . . know . . . what . . . you're saying, Mother?" She demanded, measuring every word. She stared unwaveringly, challengingly into her eyes.

Iris said nothing, just stared implacably. Irina took a step closer, another few inches and they would have been nose to nose.

"This is all nothing," Larry said nervously. "When all's said and done, Iris, how Irina deals with a suitor is Irina's affair."

"Defend her against me," her mother said bitterly.

Lower your gaze, Irina willed, *bend your head, submit!*

"If, Mother, "she said in a low, threatening voice, "you are saying what I think you're saying, I will leave this house. For good."

Staring into her eyes, Irina thought, *You know, don't you? You know everything and you don't dare face it. If I go, he goes. And you don't dare bring it to a head. You don't dare let yourself say the words out loud. You'll say what I want you to say and what you wish were so. I* WILL *it. I* WILL *it.*

"Well, mother, shall I go?"

Her mother frowned, blinked and shook her head.

"I said more than I meant. You misinterpreted what I meant. We're both too emotional. We need a drink. All of us."

110

Irina flashed Larry a sly, gloating smile, and the moment her mother turned to go to the bar Irina swung around and kissed Larry on the mouth, her heart pounding with excitement.

The swish of her motion must have been audible. Larry was horrified at her boldness. Something in her lusted to make it nakedly clear to her mother. Her mother didn't turn around. Irina joined her gaily at the bar, hugged her around the waist and kissed her cheek . . . patronizingly.

"Let me fix the drinks, and, darlings, forgive me if I caused trouble between you. Kiss and make up, you two, h'm? Purty please."

Two drinks later her mother was relaxed and fairly kittenish and Larry was being very warm to her. And, Irina noted, her mother's wish not to believe gradually overpowered her senses and she had an idea, obviously, that she was going to have a lover that night. Irina yawned and stretched voluptuously.

"I'm going on up to bed." She hugged her mother and kissed her cheek. She went to Larry and kissing him whispered, "I'll expect you—in good shape."

He no longer slept in the master bedroom. The convenient technical reason was that he needed the air conditioner, which Iris couldn't stand. So Irina shut her own door and proceeded as usual to the guest room, which she and Larry used almost every night. She stripped down naked, then put on a single garment, a wisp of net panty dotted with tiny silk roses.

When Larry came in, looking nervous and hurried, Irina was between the silk bedsheets, covered to the chin. His eyes were troubled, as he came quickly to the bed. She began to smile at him and to move herself slowly and sinuously, undulating and arching subtly, her legs gliding with a soft friction on the silk below.

The loose silk covering above dimpled and puffed and settled intriguingly, fitting softly to the contours of her body. The seductiveness pained rather than excited him.

He sat on the edge of the bed and said in a rushed, apologetic tone, "I can't stay. She's expecting me back directly."

"Don't you want to see my surprise? My new panties?"

"Darling, you know I do. But you see—"

111

She uncovered herself down to mid-thigh. She recovered herself at once, giving him a flash glimpse of her nakedness and the titillating panties.

"I only got the panties because I knew they'd please you. I've been laying here waiting for you to see them and touch and . . . then do what you want to. But you promised to sleep with her, h'm? Is that it? That's what you plan to do? Choose to do?"

"Irina, dearest. I love you. That's the truth of it; you know that. I'd choose you, if it came to a final *choice.*"

"It did, Larry." She rolled on her side away from him.

"Irina," he begged, "surely you understand."

"I won't share you. It's me or her. Right now. I don't care what she thinks. I don't want you coming to me and making excuses. Make them to her."

"Please turn and look at me, darling. I can't do this to the woman. You can't want me to. What's the point? It's liable to wreck everything. Do you want to do that?"

"I don't care." She yanked the sheet away, and just lay there, uncovered. "Are you looking at me, Larry?"

"You'll be back here in five minutes?"

"Yes."

With few exceptions Larry made love to her every night. Night and day she made herself desirable and emotionally satisfying. His workday began at home where he "breakfasted with briefcase," reading business reports and summaries, making notations while he ate. He'd never wanted distraction at that time. Anyone trying to join him was frozen out, except Irina.

From the first year Irina had known Larry she'd enjoyed simply being in his presence while he was soberly absorbed in important affairs. She would arrive, dainty in a fresh dress and seat herself demurely. If he acknowledged her presence, she would smile and speak briefly. Usually she said nothing, did nothing to bother him. She took care as she ate to present a graceful, mannerly picture, so that when he rested his eyes and his fraction-of-a-second glance touched her, she would be pleasing. She watched him unobtrusively, letting her gaze stroke lightly across him, staring only when she was positive he didn't see her.

She knew his hands and every feature of his face in detail, and she knew his subtlest shadings of expression. The virile feel of him, the dynamic force of his intelli-

112

gence encompassed her like a total atmosphere that surrounded her, she had sometimes felt, wherever she went.

Finally the moment would come when he snapped the briefcase shut and he gave his whole attention to her and she would glow with life and tell him with her eyes how she adored being his daughter, his favorite.

Now that she was totally his, she wove that deep bond of the past in with the present, getting up early for breakfast, going with him on the morning walk he liked, driving with him and the chauffeur to his train, then in the evening meeting his train. They talked about whatever he wanted to talk about.

For years, during all her vacations she'd been his lone audience in the mornings and often, too, for odd minutes or half-hours in the afternoons or evenings. He'd usually make running commentaries on things in general. At other times he'd sense things were plaguing her and make her talk, fetching her troubles out of her, absorbing and banishing them, making the world right. As she'd grown a little older, there were sessions when they both talked and debated, even argued on high planes of abstraction, and Larry had made the world sing along with new meanings.

She wanted his world to sing now. She stimulated and refreshed his senses with endless variety, experimenting with hair styles and makeup. She bought rackfuls of new clothes, smart and simple, formal and casual, bizarre and plain. She whetted him with brilliant, dazzling patterns, jewelry and perfumes; she soothed him with unornamented little pastel outfits.

She prowled the "mistress" shops in the city for spicy, intimate underthings and nightgowns. She bought expensive lingerie to delight him with her seductively veiled nudity; with the aid of salons and a personal maid she kept her body exquisite for him. When they were among outsiders socially she never flirted, but she didn't totally reject the male interest she always attracted. After one such evening Larry was moody, and finally accused her of teasing him.

"Oh, no," she assured him. She hugged and petted him, lavished kisses on him. "I didn't want to make you jealous, darling. If I want you to know other men look at me, it's not to upset you. It's to assure you, to make you see how desirable I am, to make you proud that I'm yours.

Everything I think and feel and do, Larry, is to make myself satisfying to you so you'll always be glad and never, never sorry that you own me. Own me *completely!"*

As their affair continued, she loved him more and more. She wanted to give him everything, and in turn she was a demanding mistress, using up his total sexual energies, as far as she knew, so he would have nothing left over for *anyone* else.

The sexual pleasures were only part of the satisfactions. She loved the mockery she was making of all the surfaces and conventions of life. To present the idyllically innocent front, to outhypocrite the hypocrites while feasting on forbidden fruits and violating taboos and deceiving and betraying was luscious.

And best of all was the sweet taste of an obscure revenge and the bitter look of the victim. Her mother sleepwalked, but unlike Don Colby, she had to fight to stay asleep. She distracted herself in many of the same ways she'd always done—filling her hours with cards, parties, gossip and committee work. And lately, since she'd become a grandmother, she'd displayed intense maternalism toward Elly and the baby. And all the while she resisted the awareness of what had happened to her world and her place in it.

That awareness dripped, dripped like an acid in her. Day by day she alternated between doubt and certainty of a horror. Irina watched with an almost objective fascination as her mother changed and her will began, flake by flake, to disintegrate, and her spirit sickened.

There were times when none of this showed. And there were other, sharply exciting moments when the panic and the suppressed rage and the desperation came boilingly close to the surface. Then again she would be composed, but always, always, Irina knew, the pain and knowledge of defeat was there inside, eating her alive, warping her mind, changing her image of herself, destroying her! *The queen is dead, long live the queen,* Irina thought.

Without seeming to disrupt the established order she reshaped what had been her mother's household to fit herself. Her mother's grip loosened, her interest waned and the staff of servants had come to look to Irina for orders. Their loyalty was assured by the simplest of stratagems: lavish bonuses. What they knew or suspected they kept to themselves.

But her mother's personal maid was a stronghold. She provided more than intimate service; she was practically worshipful, and she gave Iris an incalculable sense of security. A week after Irina's birthday she spoke casually to her mother about the woman.

"Mother, I don't seem to be able to find a satisfactory personal maid. Yours has always been so marvelous, I was wondering if I might borrow her. Or better, exchange her for mine."

"She's never taken to you, Irina."

"I know. She doesn't like to serve me. But she'll learn."

"No. She'd feel humiliated. We can't do that to her. She's been with me years and years."

"I'll see what she says to a doubled salary and a thousand-dollar bonus," Irina said flatly.

"You don't want her," she cried. "You just want her to take her away from me. That's it. Isn't it?"

"I want her. I can use her. I intend to use her. If she doesn't like it, she can refuse. Then I'll just have Larry speak to her."

"Don't you dare!" her mother shouted. "*I'll* speak to him, too. You'll see if you get your way on this point!"

"You're so hysterical. You'd think I was going to speak to Larry about getting Noel fired."

"What? What's that mean? What kind of talk is that?"

"I just used it as an example of something important enough to waste emotion on."

"Well, that's all it had better be. Don't you threaten me like that."

"You're shaking. Honestly, Mother! What if he did get fired? He's got a couple of million, same as me, same as Elly. He'd starve?"

"That's not what worries me. You know very well he's got to prove *himself*. It would shatter the boy if . . . well, you're not to cause trouble for him with Larry. Is that understood?"

"It's always been understood," Irina said heatedly. "You've got only one child. All your love went to him. Now, as always, you defend him like a tigress."

"You've tried to make me feel guilty all your life. Damn it, you got your share of me."

"I did not!" Irina's face colored, tightened into a scowl. "No! Well, I'm glad I didn't experience your *smotherhood*. Or I might be in the same spineless shape your only child is today. A pretentious incompetent hanging onto his mummy's husband, looking to mummy for protection. That's the only reason you're holding onto Larry when you never did love him."

"Shut up."

"All right. You don't want to hear. I don't blame you. I wouldn't want to know about it either if I'd done your kind of job of mothering. And wifing!"

"You can't be this cold, this hard, this . . . Honey, what's *happened* to you?"

"Don't honey me . . . don't *touch* me!" Irina suddenly shrieked. She backed off, glaring. Her mother turned pale.

"Baby," she cried. "You really *hate* me. . . ." Her mother's eyes began to fill with tears. Irina just looked icily at her. Her mother begged. "What did I ever *do* to you?"

"You hated me."

"No . . . No . . . Oh, I can't understand you, Irina. Why were you always this way—so mean and loving, up and down, almost all at the same time? I've thought and thought, could something have happened to you, some terrible traumatic experience I never knew about? Things happen to very young children that scare them. I remember we had a governess when you were, I think, four. Years later I heard from another family that she'd sexually abused their little girl. Did anything happen to you?"

"No!"

"Her name was Miss Burkhardt."

"I don't remember a Miss Burkhardt. What did she do to the little girl you're talking about?"

"It's quite terrible. She committed lesbian-type abuses, overstimulating her into terrible states. And there was another horrid factor. The woman was a masochistic pervert who craved abuse and she taught the girl to beat her and to take pleasure in doing it. And this was associated with sexual stimulation. Well—" her mother cringed— "it was a dreadful sort of conditioning, sadistic pleasure along with premature sexual stimulations. Fortunately she was caught and committed. I pray her sickness hadn't developed when she had you children in charge."

Irina walked away, frowning and shaking her head, trying to remember Miss Burkhardt. Finally she did, but only as an ordinary, strict governess.

116

"I do remember Miss Burkhardt."

"And—?" her mother seemed to hold her breath.

"And nothing." Irina shrugged. "Your prayer's answered. She didn't have that sickness then, as far as I know. You might ask Elly and Noel if she did anything like that to them."

"I've asked. She didn't." Her mother sighed with relief. "You've got too good a memory to have forgotten anything like that."

Irina smiled and said sunnily, "Mother, forget I mentioned it about that personal maid of yours."

"All right," she said. After a moment her mother added hesitantly, "You *are* dropping it, aren't you?"

"Yes."

"I don't want you bothering her," she said, watching Irina suspiciously. "Or trying to bribe her, as you have the other servants."

"If you're referring to bonuses I've given out around here, with Larry's approval, as bribes, I don't understand you, Mother. You asked me to postpone plans for a home of my own and remain a daughter to Larry. I've conscientiously tried to make this house pleasant for him. I had to assume responsibilities, to get the cooperation of servants who looked on me as a child without authority here. I had to use money to win them. Why did I do it? To make everything smooth for Larry.

"I attend to a hundred details, plan meals, buffets and parties that cater to *his* tastes. I see to it that there are always guests compatible to him on the lists. I've shifted the center of everything to him. Away from you, yes— away from you because he needs to know he's the master in his own home, not second string to clusters of cackling hens around card tables.

"You'll admit he has that right to be the most important person around here. You cut me to ribbons about my unsubmissive manner with Don Colby, remember? But you've been the soul of unsubmissiveness to Larry. My way of treating him has worked. He's happy here, isn't he? I give him the kind of daughterly love and appreciation you begged me to give him. But, now as always, it's impossible for me to please *you*. You hurt me, Mother, you hurt me."

Irina turned her back and stood rubbing her throat as if emotion-choked. There was a silence. She could feel

117

her mother's motionless uncertainty. Irina waited, suppressing a smile. Her mother's shaky ego demanded that she accept her daughter's words as truthful and innocent. Therefore she must accept Irina's reproach. Then—ah—Irina's heart quickened—her mother was coming, coming around to her, like a scolded child, repentant and seeking forgiveness.

"I didn't mean to hurt you. I'm nervous these days, Irina," she said faintly, her gaze lowered. She lifted her eyes to Irina's and tried to look into her.

"The way you're inspecting me this instant, Mother," Irina said injuredly, "shows mistrust. You can never admit you're wrong, can you? You see my way of honoring a man and you know it's succeeded. But you won't admit *your* way was wrong."

"Maybe . . . maybe I have been. . . ."

"Don't be unhappy." Irina smiled and patted her arm. "Two of Larry's friends from the office and their wives are coming for dinner."

"Tonight? But—"

"Didn't I tell you?" Irina said, knowing she hadn't. "Of course I did, Mother. Yesterday at lunch. Surely you remember. Oh, well, just so you know now." She gave her a kiss on the cheek. Then she smiled into her eyes. "Do be here and dressed before the cocktails, please? Remember last week when you were late and one couple who didn't know about you thought *I* was Larry's wife?"

She laughed; her mother laughed too loudly with her.

Think about it, Irina thought, leaving the room.

chapter ten

Her mother evidently did think about it and launched a counterattack. She began wearing wild colors and bolder styles: a bare-back, halter-neck gown with an open V plummeting between her breasts almost to her navel; toreador pants that hugged her sleek legs, soft-rolling hips and buttocks; swishy lounging pajamas; immense, voluptuous silk skirts and transparent blouses. Some of her at-home costumes brought the bedroom right out into the rest of the house.

One evening her slavelike personal maid creamed and massaged her, painted her toenails gold and sent her forth virtually naked in a smoke-thin black haremish costume. Iris came drifting through the game room giving off heat waves of sex like a concubine who had just drunk a potent aphrodisiac.

Irina, ponytailed and in purple short shorts and halter that exposed her young body stunningly, was in tense motion at the ping-pong table, fighting off Larry's 21-20 game point advantage. She didn't see her mother at first. She returned Larry's shot with a slamming placement to his backhand, and won the point.

"Whee!" she gloated, prancing on the balls of her feet. "Caught you flat-footed!"

When she saw the reason he'd missed she blinked, startled, and went down on her heels.

"Mother!" she cried, actually embarrassed. "After all, Mother!"

She sounded naïvely schoolgirlish even to herself. Her mother, gazing at Larry, ignored her, shut her out completely. Irina had a flustered sense of being reduced to childhood again; or cringing, weak and inferior, before the dreadful, unbeatable power of her mother. Irina's glance leaped to Larry.

He stood there looking at his wife, a fatuous grin on his face. His eyes skipped from the gold polish on her pretty feet to the sultry shadowing of her eye makeup to the veiled softness of her breasts to the intimate V-ing at the base of her pale, oval belly.

Then he reached out to the gold bangle that encircled her bare upper arm. He squeezed so that the metal bit lightly into her flesh, and her eyes seemed to gauze over with the pain-pleasure of his possessiveness. Iris moistened her brightly painted lips and spoke in the soft tone of a woman alone with her man.

"Larry, will this costume be suitable for the Halloween Ball at the club?"

"You think I'd let you go like *that?*" he said huskily.

"You wouldn't want another man to see me this way?"

"Are you crazy?" He squeezed the bangle a little tighter. Iris winced delicately.

119

"Whatever you say, darling." She sighed the words.

Irina was dumbstruck by the naked revelation of her mother's sexual impact. Its profound insidious power emanated like the musky-perfumed scent of her body, spreading like a will-paralyzing drug, destroying anger and every defense against it. Irina looked at this deadliest rival and tried to see an enemy whose very substance was bitter, hateful.

Instead, staring at that body, that source of her own life, she saw its flesh was sweet, sweet, *adorable*. A dizziness came over her. Her thighs quivered, her knees weakened. She suddenly turned away, wild-eyed. In another minute she would have sunk to the floor and buried her face against that soft, warm belly, kissing passionately . . . weeping. . . .

She rammed her arms into her loafer smock, belted it, and turned back to them. Her mother stood smiling at her, her eyes steady and hard.

Irina mumbled, half coherently. ". . . my room . . . some things . . . g'night . . ."

Larry turned a bright, blind grin to her which gradually focused, and though the mouth stayed jolly, the eyes became anxious.

"So early?" he protested. "Must you?"

"Let her go," her mother said tonelessly.

"Yes . . ." Irina fled to her room.

She lay in bed, her head aching horribly, knowing that Larry was at that moment making love to her mother. She rolled in an agony of jealousy and confused passionate cravings, wanting to be the lover in that bed, and the beloved, too—the lover and the beloved—*I love you, I hate you,* she whispered silently in the dark—to her—to him. *Love me . . . hate me . . . give me life . . . kill me!*

She couldn't stand it. She felt feverish. She felt chilled. Her breasts ached. Tears scalded her eyes, crawled, chilling, onto her cheeks and temple. She had to go away and there was nowhere to go. The world away from here was empty of meaning, full of terror.

Larry crept into her room late and sat there petting her, apologizing, explaining that he loved her. He expected reproaches; she had none. She just sat with her arms around him and held to him passionately, crying silently, hating herself.

He came to her the next night, and was her lover, ten-

120

der and powerful and commanding. She lay beneath his strong body sheltered by his goodness, feeling the bliss of his virile man flesh fused with her woman flesh. She kissed his body, loving him.

Afterward she lay sleepless half the night. Finally she woke Larry.

"You're mine," she whispered. "My rightful mate. It's torture to think of sharing you. She doesn't love you first in the whole world the way I do. She just wants to get you back to beat me. I won't let her. I won't. Do you hear?"

"Calm down, sweetheart, it's all right."

"It's not. She knows. She's fighting me. She'll get you again. She did before. I'm nothing against her."

"You're *everything!*" he said harshly. "I'd divorce her, marry you in a minute, but I can't quite subject her to that public humiliation. Meantime, she doesn't know it's you."

"She must."

"No. She believes I'm seeing someone in the city in the daytime."

"Why did you tell her a thing like that?"

"Surely you don't *want* her to know."

"The hell I don't. I want the whole world to know. I don't want to be a swept-under-the-rug dirty secret thing to you. I want to stand up and shout it."

"Well, you're not going to. Stop this hysteria this instant. Do you hear me?"

"Yes."

"No more of that!"

"I'm done, darling. It's over." She kissed and stroked him. "I'll be good. I haven't made you unhappy, have I?"

"No."

"Please make love to me."

"I'm tired. Get back to sleep. Turn over. Go on. I mean it, Irina."

"Yes." She turned and lay spooned in against him. He patted and soothed her and lay with his cheek against her head so that she could feel him smiling and she squirmed and sighed and slept.

The third Sunday in October was at the bleak edge of winter, but the bright, warm weather, like everything else, had a deceptive, glossy perfection about it. People kept dropping in for drinks and to offer banalities about the autumn-leaf view of the countryside from the hilltop and to pay sentimental homage to Elly's baby.

Everyone was outside most of the afternoon, playing games on the lawn, lounging with drinks in the sun, snacking from the buffet, strolling the paths down around the pond or swimming. The air sang with laughter and affectionate banter. Irina, bare-legged in a colorful, swirly skirt, net blouse and with gay ribbons in her hair, darted all over the place, looking as light as fluff, her smile quick-flashing, her talk teasy-sweet. But her eyes were watchful, her inner mood a seething anger.

Don Colby, scraggly in walking shorts, tried to be amiable and confident. Imagining he pleased her by acting like he was already part of the family, he cozied with Noel, praised Elly the Mother, made coy remarks about starting a family. He calculated his every word and action to disarm her. When she withheld approval he lost confidence.

"You look like an overgrown, disoriented campfire boy. Quit following me around and watching everything I do."

"But darling, last night you were so *loving.* . . ."

"Because I rolled strawberries in cream and sugar and fed you from my fingers? Do you know how silly you looked to Larry?"

"But, doll, you were silly, too. It was fun. Cute and—"

"Childish! I never get a feeling you've got the substance a woman can lean on. Can you imagine Larry letting a woman make him ridiculous in public? And look at you in short pants. Larry and most of the men are in slacks. But you!"

"Larry . . . Larry . . . Larry! That's all I hear from you!"

He went sulking into the house and reappeared in long pants. Every time she got near Larry Don began nibbling his mustache and hustled over to them. Between times he watched her compulsively—maybe, she thought indifferently, with the same anxiety that she watched Larry.

Larry was acting entirely too lord-of-the-manor satisfied with the pretty-picture surface life he was living. Richly tanned and buoyant and looking handsome in the imported shoes, tailored slacks and silk casual shirt Irina had bought for him, he strolled around immensely pleased with himself.

He fed on his wife's smiles and made proud remarks about "his" grandchild and on three occasions he put his arm around Elly the Mother's waist and strolled with her. He walked-talked man-to-man with Noel, discussing things "down at the shop," as Noel liked to put it. Larry stood with Noel in a ring of his mother's friends and puffed Noel's fat head fatter with praise of his professional abilities.

Noel's sense of well-being, Irina observed narrowly, was nothing to his mother's bliss. Iris affected a limply contented air; even to her bouffant hair style which diminished and softened her face. She kept giving Larry melted-eyed looks and taking occasions to lace her arm with his or twine her fingers possessively about his hand.

"She handles you," Irina said in a rushed, hoarse voice when she got Larry alone, "as if she really owns you. And you not only don't discourage that impression, you publicly proclaim it."

"The appearance is little enough to give her, sweetheart. After all, *we* have the reality." He gazed at her gently. "You're trembling, your fingers are cold."

"She's pulled you into that circle. And you're moving into it willingly. Leaving me out here!"

"You're the center. You know it. Stop being frightened."

"I can't help it. Look at all the things she's got to give you there in that cozy domestic circle—a son, a daughter, a granddaughter, friends, pride—all these things you want and need and that I can't give you. . . ." She caught her breath and began to blink back tears. "They've got everything, all the nice, calm, sweet virtues. And what am I? Ugly. No good. I can't give any more than a whore could. You're beginning to go to their side and . . . and . . ."

"Let's walk," he said, gripping her arm. "Keep moving. Smile. Don't cry—*don't,* baby! I love you more than all of them put together!"

Walking with him she calmed a little.

"Damn," Larry said, "here comes that Colby fellow."

"What if I should publicly proclaim and honor him? Show the world that the appearance is true, that I love *him*. I should. I should marry him!"

123

"Don't say that, Irina. Please!"

"I should, Larry. And start a family so that you can publicly proclaim me before the world as you did Elly. I could give you a grandchild to be proud of and have a home and respectability and you'd honor *me* before the world."

"Colby might hear you," Larry warned. "Shut up. We'll go into it later. . . . How're you there, Don?"

"Hi, Larry," Colby said, looking anxiously at him, then at Irina. "We were getting up a doubles game . . . uh . . ."

"I was just coming for you to go with me to see about getting the fire going and the steaks out to the broilers." She smiled and took his hand and squeezed affectionately and Don brightened. Going off with him, she glanced back to see Larry watching her unhappily.

Don had finished his elaborate good-byes that night and Irina had started out to the car to drive him to the train when she heard him remark, "Hope your trip's successful, Larry."

"Thanks, Don."

"What trip?" Irina said, coming back.

Her mother, standing with an arm around Larry's waist, gave her a feline smile.

"Business trip," she said condescendingly. "Nothing to worry your pretty little head about. You kids run along now. And remember what I told you, Don?"

He grinned and winked. On the road he spoke in a firm voice.

"You're driving too fast for this road. Slow down, Irina."

"Did she instruct you to get manly with me?" she demanded.

"It's the only way to handle you."

Irina increased the speed. "This cat's got sharp claws, Don Colby. Don't fool with me."

"Fool with you? I *love* you. I need you. I can't go on without you. Marry me. Or . . ."

"Or what?"

"Please, Irina."

She said nothing. At the depot she came to a skidding stop.

"We were going to have a half-hour together. Not now. Get out. Wait for the train by yourself."

"Irina, you can't treat me—"

"Get out!" she said fiercely.

"You're so beautiful I could—"

"Get out!"

"No. Please. Say you'll marry me."

"If you don't do what I tell you you'll never see me again!"

She finally got rid of him and raced back home. She saw a light in the bathroom of the master bedroom. She rushed into the house. Larry was on the stairs.

"Surprise!" she yelled. "I'm back fast. Too quick for you to sneak in a bed session with her."

He hurried down, frowning, a finger to his lips.

"Don't shush me!" she cried. He tried to embrace her. She twisted away and backed off, shaking her head. "I didn't know about any trip. When?"

"Tomorrow afternoon," he whispered. "A few days in Chicago. Purely business. I'm going alone."

"You didn't tell me!" she accused. "But *she* knew."

"I haven't had the chance. Colby came out on the train Friday with me. You and I've hardly had a minute together."

"Excuses! Lies! Tonight you were going to her. Tomorrow night, without any warning to me, you'd be gone."

"I was going to tell you tonight. Be reasonable."

"Reasonable!" she said bitterly.

"Larry?" Her mother appeared at the head of the stairs. "What's going on down there?"

"Irina's back."

"So I hear." Her mother came part way down, peering at them. She was in a negligee. "It's late, Larry. Come to bed."

"A minute, Iris." He looked torn. "She had a fight with Colby."

"That's her problem. Are you coming?"

Irina looked at him starkly.

"If you go now, Larry," she said quietly, "you'll be sorry."

He took it as a threat and his eyes flashed with anger and his jaw became blocky. She realized too late that she wasn't talking to Don Colby, but to a man who wouldn't be pushed around. He glanced up the stairs.

"Coming right up, Iris. . . . Irina, this is a problem you're adult enough to handle. All you have to use is

125

your head." He took her by the shoulders, gave her a chaste kiss on the forehead. "Good night," he said, and turned away.

"Good night, Irina," her mother called down sweetly.

"Good night, Mother," she said coolly, without looking up. "Good night, Larry. Enjoy your trip."

"Thanks, dear."

"Where'll you be staying?"

He paused and gazed down at her unsmilingly.

"The Graystone."

Five days later she placed a long-distance call to the Graystone. It was past midnight and Larry was in his suite.

"Hi, Larry."

"Irina! Where are you? Where've you been? I've phoned home daily. Your mother doesn't know. What're you trying to do, worry me to death?"

"Of course not, Larry," she said gaily. "I'm fine. I'm in Florida."

"Well, catch the next plane home and I'll see you tomorrow."

"I can't. I'm staying here."

"Then I'll fly down there. Give me your address, honey. I can't stand us being angry. I know I hurt you. I'm sorry. I'll make it all up to you, dearest."

"You're so nice, Larry. Don'll just be delighted to know you're coming. I bet you give us the *nicest* wedding present!"

"What? You're not going to *marry* him, for God's sake!"

"No," she said, grinning. She paused. "I already did."

"You don't mean it, Irina. Don't tease me like that. Irina. Stop it. Damnit," he said with rising agitation, *"it's not true!"*

"Don's down in the bar. Do you want to have him paged so you can ask him?"

There was a long, terrible silence, then an odd sound.

"Larry?" she whispered. Did I hear you cry? Did you love me that much?"

"How could you do this to me?" he said brokenly.

She started to cry, too.

"I've got to hang up, Larry."

"I guess you'd better."

She couldn't. She sat crying miserably.

126

"I hurt as much as you do, Larry. But it's got to be this way."

"I've got to see you, Irina . . . I'm coming."

"*No*. Don't come. We'll be *gone*. Good-bye, Larry."

"I love you!"

"Good-bye, Larry!" She hung up. She rolled over and sobbed into the pillow.

chapter eleven

It was Don's dismal performance—rather, nonperformance—in bed after their little wedding supper in the suite that had driven him down to the bar. When he returned about two in the morning, Irina feigned sleep and watched him through meshed eyelashes.

Staggering drunk, he mumbled endearments and apologies to her, then supposing she was asleep, he tiptoed around getting himself noisily undressed in a series of sprawls and recoveries. He bent down to kiss her cheek and nearly fell on her, and started for the other bed. Then he paused at the foot of her bed and stared slackmouthed at her motionless figure.

He hadn't switched off the lamps and she could clearly see the sly transformation of his face. He began to grin and leer. He sobered, casting a quick guilty glance back across his shoulder. He looked at her again and began furtively to loosen the covers at the end of the bed. She let herself be uncovered, feeling a tremor of tension. He stood looking at her and began to frown; he grasped himself privately and his expression became harsh. He went to the switch and darkened the room.

When he came stealthily onto the bed and tried to mount her, thinking she didn't know about it, Irina felt a cold shiver over her skin. He made grunting or growling sounds while he tried to use her and she remained as inert as—she felt a chill—as a corpse. He was inert, too, and couldn't penetrate. She stirred, letting him know she was awake.

"Sweetheart," he said, fawningly, "I love you so much."

"But, darling, you're too drunk right now. Go to sleep."

When he was safely in the other bed she felt nauseated.

By the time he woke next morning Irina had made travel arrangements for them to the Bahamas. From there they flew to the Virgin Islands, to Puerto Rico, to Florida again, New Orleans. The month-long honeymoon hop-skipped to nine places, finishing at an island off the Carolinas. Forwarded telegrams and special delivery letters from Larry chased them throughout; others awaited them at Don's bachelor apartment in New York. Meantime she and Don did have a sexual life, but of a sort that made it almost impossible for them to look one another in the eye in daylight.

On their wedding night he'd been afraid of being an inadequate lover. With good reason! He's lain caressing and fondling and kissing her till she was on fire and past fire and on fire again. All the while he remained at a temperature almost indistinguishable from death. He wanted to do all the loving; he didn't want to be loved.

Her attempts to caress him made him shrink with embarrassment and lose all the faint fervor he'd achieved. At last, their third or fourth night together he hoarded his total passion and flung it away like a spendthrift. He was in and out like a sneakthief. But at least he'd functioned. She hoped that he'd broken some block by the act and it would be better in the future.

It wasn't. He wanted her seldom. He never satisfied her or himself. A sense of loyalty made Irina reject comparisons but after Larry, Don, the "lover," was impossible. She became increasingly dissatisfied. She could feel her marriage breaking up before it had got off the ground. He shunted off all talk about it and she couldn't reach him with words. Not entirely by accident, she found the solution. She lost her temper.

She'd been lying there being caressed and suddenly she sat up in bed and hit him. She leaped on him and slapped him in the face, left-right, left-right, fast and hard. He lay on his back taking it. She straddled his chest, thrust her face close above his and began to call him every vile name she could think of.

He didn't lift a hand, just lay under her staring up in the dark. She yanked out some of his chest hair. She slapped him viciously again, then put her palm to his lips to be

128

kissed. And he kissed. And he was panting and sexually aroused and he started to roll her over on her back.

"Stay there!' she commanded in a hiss. "On your back."

They made love then, and nightly thereafter, in that position, Don always beneath her. All she had to do was hurt him in some way and give him the feel of being subdued and he roused fast. But in the daytime he couldn't look at her directly. Only in darkness or half-light would he show himself.

Sometimes she would take a cigarette and burn him, staring down at him while he squirmed and sweat broke out and he suffered while she inflicted. Sometimes she made him lie on the floor and walked on him and kicked him and he was liable to seize her foot and shower it with kisses just as he did her hand when *it* had hurt him.

Irina loved the look of genuine pain on his face when he was being really hurt. She loved the mood of him when they stood naked by the bed and she would order him onto the bed and he would crawl on and lie supine. He loved it. *And hated it.*

She wondered if she hadn't always instinctively known there was something a trifle "off" about him? Maybe the queerness had been the key to her hanging onto him, never totally rejecting him? Hadn't she expected from marriage the kind of satisfaction his masochism had provided? Yes! She would get no sexual kick out of him as a normal lover. He'd be dull, hopelessly dull.

Larry's bombardment of telegrams, though not too nakedly clear, was an agony to Don. Her answer to his furiously jealous questions about her and Larry was simple.

"Shut up!"

And she would stare unwaveringly into his eyes until he dropped or shifted his gaze.

At first, till she found the big New Jersey house, they lived in Don's bachelor apartment. The day after they returned she phoned Larry and said she wanted to have lunch with him. Wearing a new dress and hat and a mink coat and looking her prettiest, she reached the restaurant breathless with excitement.

When she saw Larry there in the outer bar she shivered from head to toe. He made his way to her. His face looked drained, wooden. Only his eyes were alive with yearning.

"Irina!" he said tenderly. He clasped both her hands in his and gazed down at her. "You're not happy."

"No," she whispered, her breasts aching.

"Our table's waiting. We'll have a drink there."

"I can't eat." She could hardly breathe. She closed her eyes, gripped his hands. "I just want you."

"I'll get my coat. Wait."

"No." She went with him to the cloakroom, then outside and into a cab and rode along the avenue, feeling faint. She sat tense beside him. Waves of desire began to sweep through her. In the elevator of his apartment building he kissed her and she moaned in a kind of delirium and opened her lips to him.

Inside the apartment there was a rage and worship and tenderness and harsh possessiveness about him all wrapped up together. He undressed her garment by garment, kissing her body, as if to consume her totally, and his love words poured out like a bath of passion. Then she was lying in his arms, rejoined with him in ecstasy. She wouldn't let go. They made love a second time. Then, after sleep, a third. She reached home long after dark.

"Where were you?" Don demanded, his eyes burning with accusation.

"Out."

"You've been with another man."

"You can eliminate the word 'another.' " She went to the closet, hung up her coat, came out and began indifferently to remove her dress.

"Meaning you've been with a man and I'm not one? I know *who*, by God!"

"Shut up! You don't know anything." She removed a brooch and let it fall to her feet. She glanced down at it, unmoving, then up into Don's eyes, her command silent.

His face began to color; he blinked excitedly and wet his lips. He dropped to his knees, picked up the brooch, then gazed up at her, waiting.

Expressionless, Irina said, "While you're down there, take off my shoes." She slapped his face as hard as she could. He seized her hand and kissed the palm. For a moment she allowed it, then yanked her hand away and extended her foot. He bent to it. She stood over him, her lip curled faintly, her eyes glittering.

A week later Larry dragooned her mother into an evening on the town with her and Don. At dinner Larry

130

and her mother jointly presented them with a generous check as a wedding gift and her mother's smiling mask was in place. It remained there till the second intermission at the play, when Larry, bringing drinks for them, could not disguise the way he felt when he looked at Irina. From then on her mother didn't say another word to Irina directly. In the night club she and Don both got tipsy and danced with each other, leaving Larry and Irina alone at the table.

"It's not working," Larry confided huskily. "Even when we don't look at or speak to each other, dearest, the love between us screams, and it's torturing her."

"Then it'll have to be secret."

Every time her mother could bear to look at her, there was a sort of draining and fading about her face and an expression of pain in her eyes that touched Irina with a throat-clutching anguish, and at the same time stirred up a gloating, malevolent joy. It wasn't necessary for her mother to believe there was an actual affair between her husband and her daughter. It was quite enough that she see that Larry craved her blindly.

Irina couldn't help remembering the feline smile her mother had given her that last Sunday night at home, and before the painful evening on the town was done Irina gave that smile back to her *twice*.

In early December they leased the New Jersey country place. The house sat within several acres of woods-fringed land and under the snow, the agent assured, showing them summery color pictures, were velvety, undulating lawns, flowered terraces, tennis and badminton courts, putting green, a vast grill in a shady picnic-area. The glass-brick and pale stone eighteen-room house formed a wide-based U framing a pool-patio area for dancing and outdoor parties in season.

Irina spent over a month refurnishing, redecorating and hiring the staff. The sitting room was vast, centered by a hooded fireplace. The jewel piece was a circular bedroom; part of its arc was a window wall with an unbroken view to the woods at the property line.

Leading off the perimeter of the circular bedroom was an ornate, bright-mirrored bath-dressing room and wardrobe, a maid's room, and on the other side a bedroom for Don. There was an eight-foot circular bed on which she planned to sleep alone there in the center of a ring of cool free space, with a servant at her beck and call from one point, a slave from another. The ceiling, walls and drapes were sky-blue, the thick carpet sun-yellow; the spread on the big, round bed matched the carpet so that bed appeared to be a raised section of the floor.

The night of the day they moved in Irina retired early after dinner, promising Don she would be nice to him. She bathed languorously. She lay afterward on the vibrator massage table while her maid brushed her hair, then stroked lotion on her body and finally did her nails, hands and feet. Stepping into fur slippers Irina went into the big room. She unlocked Don's door, then reclined stark-naked on the bed with the lights blazing.

"Don!" she called. Then louder. *"Don!"*

He appeared, ready in pajamas. The sight of her shocked his senses joyously. He stood there feasting on the sight of her.

"God," he breathed, "you're a jewel. A jewel."

She lifted one long leg, extended her foot and teased her toes against his body, smiling voluptuously.

"Love me," she purred. He started toward the light switch. "No, Don. With the lights on."

She lay smiling, watching in the mirror as he worshiped her like an idol.

When he was done she lay in the dark thinking about Larry. She hadn't seen him for two weeks and he was frantic. She knew because she'd been phoning him regularly, teasing him, refusing to see him. Not because she didn't want to, but he was too sure of her and needed a lesson. She tiptoed across the room, locked Don's door, got her phone and brought it back to the bed. She dialed home. Her mother answered.

Irina breathed close to the mouthpiece.

"Who is this?"

Irina grinned, said nothing, just breathed close to the phone so she could hear.

"It's you, Irina, isn't it? You devil. You devil. He's there with you, isn't he? That's why he stayed in town."

Irina hung up. She dialed his city apartment. He didn't answer. She got up and made herself a drink and phoned again in an hour. Still no answer. At one o'clock he answered.

"I was going to come to you tonight," she said. "But I guess you've had your fun."

"Irina, where are you? I must see you."

"I'm home. Don't you wish you knew where that was?"

She laughed softly and hung up. It turned out that he did know where she lived. He'd hired detectives. He came in person next morning. Stress lines showed on his broad face and his eyes had a jumpiness about them she'd never seen before.

"Can I come in?"

"Of course," she said. "We're having open house in a week, but if you want a preview. . . ."

She was in a voluminous house coat and as she sat on a sofa across from him in the front room she let it fall away briefly, showing herself bare underneath.

"Can't we be alone somewhere?"

"Such as a bedroom?" she laughed. "All right, come along. I'll *show* you my bedroom."

She did just that, then gave him a tour of the rest of the house.

"I'm a contented and faithful wife now, Larry. I can't allow you to come here any more."

She said it in one way and another for the next two hours until finally, when she dressed and had lunch there with him, he began to believe it. When he left, walking dejectedly, she accompanied him to the car and gave him a daughterly cheek kiss.

"You and mother must be here for the open house."

"You know she won't come. Shall I, anyhow?"

"If you like. You can meet some of Don's family and friends. No, don't look at me that way, Larry. We're done. That's all there is to it. After the open house I'm going up to Vermont for some skiing."

Three nights later she had a surprise for him. She was sitting naked on the dresser bench in his apartment. He came at her like a starving man and began to kiss her. For the next week or so she let him have her. Then she vanished for two weeks of skiing.

When she returned to the city she checked in at the Plaza and phoned his office. He was at a board meeting and they didn't put the call through. It was three hours before he knew she'd phoned and returned her call. He started apologizing at once.

She cut him off. "I'm going to check out in twenty minutes."

"Make it two hours. I'll be there then. I have a very important appointment in a half-hour, downtown."

"See you next time I'm in the city, Larry."

"Wait."

She hung up and she went down to the lobby and watched the clock. In twenty-five minutes Larry came hurrying to the desk, his face darkly anxious. Seeing her, he beamed.

"I was able to switch the time on the apointment!"

"Good! You darling! Shall we go up?"

Later there were times when he couldn't swing things so simply. If he wanted her he had to make a hard choice and the strain began to tell.

"You're drinking too much these days, Larry," Irina observed one afternoon at cocktails. "You're haggard."

"Business."

"You're not neglecting it, are you? Losing your grasp?"

"I dunno. And I don't care." He laughed foolishly and quoted, "The world is well lost for love!"

"If it's doing this to you, Larry, I'm done. Really done."

He lost his temper. "Damn it, there you go again! Threatening to leave me high and dry. I don't know where I am with you or anything else any more. Let's get out of this goddamned dive!"

"Whatever you say."

"Whatever I say! Whatever I say," he said bitterly. "Submissive you. Worshipful you. Looking up at me on a pedestal, and sawing it out from under me at the same time!"

He continued word-lashing her and himself on the way back to the apartment, making her cry. But he kept drinking and after a while his anger dissolved.

"Ah, what's it matter whether it's poison or not, I've got to have it. I don't give a damn about anything else but you. Leave that masochist bastard, Irina."

"He doesn't exist."

"Yes. Don feeds your sadism. He's poisoning you. And worse, baby, there's something I worry about—the nature of masochism. It's the twin of sadism. It's liable to turn its other face at any time. It's at your feet now, tomorrow it's at your throat. Leave him."

"Forget him," she said with a careless wave of her arm.

"I'm going to forget *you* instead, Irina. By God, I'm *resolved.*"

He became suddenly grim. She looked at him blankly. "All right, Larry, let's try it that way."

He held out for six or seven weeks. She guessed what had happened. Then she checked and saw for herself that he had a new mistress. A green-eyed, swish-tailed, little redhead who affected purple eye shadow and had the cheap trick of licking her upper lip provocatively when she was gazing at him in a shadowy bar booth.

The two of them came to his apartment from a club at three A.M. one Saturday morning. Larry opened the door and didn't know anybody was inside and he walked his redhead in.

The next thing the girl knew she had a fist in one eye, another in her belly. Then she was on her back screaming and kicking her naked legs while Irina sat on her and beat her face with her fists trying to make her whole face match the purple eyelids. While Larry was trying, and finally succeeding in pulling Irina off, she ripped the bitch's dress open, tore off her bra and flung her foam rubber charms across the room.

After she'd got rid of the slut she made love to Larry till he was wild with desire, then she ran out, leaving him unsatisfied and in misery.

The week before Don's birthday in June Irina told him, "I'm throwing a party for you, darling. Your family and friends. My family. I want you to phone Mother and get her to come."

"I don't know if I can. It'd have to include Larry."

"Have you still got that bug about Larry? Of course he'll come. With his wife. You're so unreasonably jealous. Haven't I been a good wife? In many ways. Sure I was gone skiing a lot of weekends and I picked up some wild characters along the way. But your friends have accepted me. And people at the club here, even your family. I do see to it that our dinners are nice. I'm nice to your people and to your business friends. I haven't given you such a bad home."

"That's so to a degree, Irina. You know how to entertain and make people feel good. When you want to." His features were somber and reflective.

135

"I want to now. And I want a reconciliation with Mother. She's a little mean. I'm a little mean. But the quality has its advantages—h'm, lover? Would you want me any other way?"

He grinned, only a trifle sheepishly, and shifted his eyes. "I'll phone your mother."

"Coax. Beg. She's crazy about you. She can't refuse to come to your birthday party."

While he made the phone call Irina sat near, looking at him rather wistfully as he turned on the charm for her mother. There seemed to be a certain amount of resistance for a few minutes, but he was persuasive. His pleasure in his success when he had hung up was really quite appealing. Irina went over and curled up on his lap and petted him.

"You know, Don, you're a lovable guy."

She resolved to make the party a real success for him. First thing tomorrow she would start the arrangements. The affair would have to be catered and it would be outside in the pool-patio area. There would be seventy or eighty guests. She'd have a live orchestra. She'd have the club social director book a professional show; maybe she'd build a stage over part of the pool. She began to visualize details, including the size of the cake and the manner of presentation. It was one of the best parties that never took place.

chapter twelve

It was Sunday morning. The servants were gone. Don was playing golf. She was to meet him for lunch at the club at two. She breakfasted at an umbrellaed table out by the pool, then sunned herself for a while.

About eleven, she put on a little bathing suit, stuffed her hair in a rubber cap and dove into the glistening turquoise pool. She swam lazily for a while, then raced herself up and down the pool several times. She climbed out, prancy and sparkling, the exertion giving her sleek, water-beaded legs a pink flush that matched her bathing suit.

She put on a white toweling robe, blotted herself and skinned off her cap, shaking her black hair out loosely, her face shiningly upturned to the sun. She heard the car with a sense of mild curiosity and stepping into scuffs went to the end of the building to see who it was.

She was surprised to see it was Larry. Involuntarily her heart picked up a beat and she experienced a quick-clenching sexual spasm, exquisite but oddly touched with anxiety. She drew a breath, lowered her eyes in almost automatic submission and walked toward him as he got out of his white convertible.

Bare-headed and wearing a tropical shirt and sunglasses, he nonetheless looked somber. Hollows ran down his cheeks and the corners of his full mouth seemed weighted. He moved toward her wearily.

"Larry, are you all right?" She reached him, took his hand and fell in beside him.

"No." He shook his head. "Is anyone home?"

"No one."

"I want you."

"Right now? Honestly, Larry, it's going to wipe out every other meaning we ever had for each other."

He stopped. "Are you just bedeviling me, or is that what you really think?"

"That's what I'm really afraid of. But what's the difference? I don't care. I want you. You want me. All right. Come on."

She led him inside and back through the cool hall and into the big circular bedroom. She slipped off bathing suit and toweling robe and lay herself out across the big round bed. He came onto the bed with her and for a while they lay on their sides, pressed to each other in a comfortable embrace.

They kissed slowly and warmed one another and then with the ease of loving familiarity they moved into position. She lay smiling up at him as he came above and prepared to possess her warm, yielding flesh. All the weariness was gone from his face and there was a joyous luster in his eyes. And then they were locked to each other, caught up in the wavelike blissful rhythm and oblivious to everything outside themselves. They reached the intensity of climax. Then there was the descent of self-consciousness and . . . *guilt,* guilt so strong it took the form of a shocking hallucination.

Irina blinked and the stunned face and staring eyes did not vanish. She clutched Larry and gave a shrill cry and he twisted around and made a hoarse, startled sound. And the hallucination remained. Her mother's face. And body, and . . . and it *wasn't* an hallucination. Suddenly her mother's face crumpled. She didn't say a word. A single, wailing, anguished cry seemed to rip from her throat and she spun around and ran hysterically.

Larry, and an instant later Irina, was up, getting into clothes. They heard Iris' car start. There was a screech of tires and then a rising engine roar. Irina and Larry looked at each other in helpless fright.

"She's out of her mind," Irina said. "Something may happen to her. Try to catch her, Larry!"

Within minutes they had both set out in separate cars. They didn't have far to drive.

At a turn in the narrow road just two miles away they found the smoking car, crashed into a culvert. The engine had come back into the seat crushing Iris' body and breaking her neck. Her head lay back as though detached; her dying agony seemed stamped into the tissue of her face. The dead eyes stared wide-open at the sky.

Irina and Larry were the first ones there. Irina began to shake helplessly. Larry covered his face.

"My God . . . my God . . . I killed her!"

Don, when he arrived thirty minutes later, after being summoned by highway police, seemed to take it harder than anyone. He cried like a baby. But then he began to harden.

Driving back home with Irina late that night he said coldly, "I know why she drove at that kind of speed. She was *driven.* And I know why. I know who drove her." He began to swear. "She didn't just come visiting our place. She followed that bastard Larry to our house and what she saw going on inside is what killed her. I don't care what *you* say!" He looked at her slashingly. "You hear me?"

"I'm sick enough. Let me alone." Irina was numb, her face ashen, a dull, tearing ache clutching and clawing at her vitals.

When they got home he poured himself a long drink. He tossed it off and then just stood glaring at her.

"You and that bastard!"

"You wouldn't call him that to his face. What kind of man are you, attacking him when he's been hit by a tragedy like this?"

She glared and left the room. She got almost to her bedroom when Don came running after her, enraged.

"What kind of a man am I, eh? You always did question that, didn't you, you bitch! Get in there, woman. Get in there on that bed."

He shoved her into the room and toward the bed. She balked and he shoved more violently and kept pushing till she was at the edge of the bed. He pushed her off balance, flopping onto the bed. He pulled off her shoes and crawling onto the bed yanked her skirt up and tore her panties down, his nails scratching her skin.

"Stop it! Damn you!" She was angry and just a little startled.

He smashed her with his fist, knocking her flat. He got up and ripped off his pants. She saw he was sexually intense. He leaped on her and when she fought he overpowered her and actually raped her.

Afterward, he continued to hold her down as if he was out of his mind. He stared glassily into her face, panting and sweating. With horror she realized he was becoming sexually vigorous again, and like an animal he tried to force himself on her. Terror began to stalk along her nerves. She looked at Don and suddenly she saw a complete stranger.

She struggled wildly to get away. He smashed her with his fists. She lost consciousness. When she came to he was still straddling her.

"Lie still. We'll wait. Then we'll have some more. . . ."

He must have held her there for an hour, intimidating her, his face a mask of savage fury, his eyes bright and hard and altogether strange.

He used her again. They lay there for she didn't know how much longer. He tried to use her and he wasn't capable.

He got up and stalked around the bed, watching her, holding her captive. Everything was out of control, she knew with a genuine sense of terror. She crouched, watching him nervously. Things were out of control. She had lost command over him and she knew stark, nerve-racking terror.

She made a sudden dash for the door. Don's fist looped out of nowhere, smashing the side of her head and knocking her to the floor. He pounced, straddling her and started to beat her face with his fists. She screamed and the scream became gauzy and remote as she lost consciousness.

She came up out of a blackness into a horrid redness; and through shattering pain she could feel slick, wet, sticky blood on her face. Don was holding a thick, shattered glass vase. She began to whimper and paw out futilely with her hands and heave her body against his weight. He gouged her face with the glass again, then there was a white-roaring agonizing explosion in her head and a long, long blackness.

When she came to again, she was alone and she got up and crawled, her eyes swollen nearly shut. She could see blood all over the carpet and there was broken glass and smashed furniture and shattered windows and the drapes were in a heap. Moving awkwardly, she stumbled over another heap and fell.

It was Don, motionless, silent. A portion of heavy mirror glass from the smashed vanity emerged like a broken sword from his upper abdomen, as if he'd fallen on it in his frenzy. When she realized he was dead she began to scream and scream and scream. . . .

There was a confusion of steps and voices and somewhere in the distance she could see a winking red light. She was being carried to an ambulance. Her shredded, ruined face was in bandages. They must have given her something for she felt no pain.

Walking beside her was a man with a sick face and he gazed at her with tragic eyes and there were tears on his cheeks.

"Irina . . . Irina . . . Irina," he kept saying in a desperate voice. "Don't you know me, Irina? Don't you know Larry?"

Then they were sliding her in the ambulance and shutting the doors and the poor unhappy man was left outside. Then the big old ambulance was moving away and the siren was whining and they were riding real fast and she yelled *whee* and giggled and then she wondered who that nice man back there had been and who Irina was. Then she forgot about that and started to sing pretty along with the ambulance siren *whooo-wheee-whooo-wheee* . . . .